TALES FROM MY BOYHOOD

Ruskin Bond is known for his signature simplistic and witty writing style. He is the author of several bestselling short stories, novellas, collections, essays and children's books; and has contributed a number of poems and articles to various magazines and anthologies. At the age of 23, he won the prestigious John Llewellyn Rhys Prize for his first novel, *The Room on the Roof*. He was also the recipient of the Padma Shri in 1999, Lifetime Achievement Award by the Delhi Government in 2012 and the Padma Bhushan in 2014.

Born in 1934, Ruskin Bond grew up in Jamnagar, Shimla, New Delhi and Dehradun. Apart from three years in the UK, he has spent all his life in India and now lives in Landour, Mussoorie, with his adopted family.

RUSKIN BOND

TALES FROM MY BOYHOOD

RUPA

Published by
Rupa Publications India Pvt. Ltd 2023
7/16, Ansari Road, Daryaganj
New Delhi 110002

Sales centres:
Bengaluru Chennai
Hyderabad Jaipur Kathmandu
Kolkata Mumbai Prayagraj

Copyright © Ruskin Bond 2023

All rights reserved.
No part of this publication may be reproduced, transmitted,
or stored in a retrieval system, in any form or by any means,
electronic, mechanical, photocopying, recording or otherwise,
without the prior permission of the publisher.

This is a work of fiction. Names, characters, places and incidents are
either the product of the author's imagination or are used
fictitiously and any resemblance to any actual person, living or
dead, events or locales is entirely coincidental.

P-ISBN: 978-93-5702-878-3
E-ISBN: 978-93-5702-797-7

First impression 2023

10 9 8 7 6 5 4 3 2 1

The moral right of the author has been asserted.

Printed in India

This book is sold subject to the condition that it shall not,
by way of trade or otherwise, be lent, resold, hired out, or otherwise
circulated, without the publisher's prior consent, in any form of
binding or cover other than that in which it is published.

CONTENTS

Introduction   vii

1. In Grandfather's Garden   1
2. The Room of Many Colours   7
3. The Last Tonga Ride   32
4. The Young Rebel   46
5. Miss Babcock's Big Toe   58
6. Breakfast at Barog   61
7. The Playing Fields of Shimla   67
8. My Father's Trees in Dehra   75
9. Friends of My Youth   87
10. How Far Is the River?   102
11. Four Boys on a Glacier   106
12. The Dehra I Know   111
13. Be Prepared   116
14. A Love of Long Ago   120
15. The Four Feathers   126
16. Here Comes Mr Oliver   131

INTRODUCTION

Looking back on our childhood days, most of us might be surprised by what our mind chooses to remember. Flashes of conversations shared with friends, lazy afternoons spent lounging at home, joyful train rides, delicious family meals or even the kindness of a stranger shine through the mist of time. These flashes are like a sweet whiff of spring in the dead of winter.

Tales from My Boyhood journeys into my childhood memories that evoke feelings of warmth and joy. Tales like 'The Playing Fields of Shimla' and 'Here Comes Mr Oliver' are a glimpse into my time at boarding school. 'The Last Tonga Ride' and 'In Grandfather's Garden' offer a window into my childhood adventures in Dehra. 'A Love of Long Ago' brings to light my first taste of love and the bittersweet moments it brings. Stories like 'Friends of My Youth' are a loving ode to some of my cherished friendships.

These stories are filled with laughter (maybe even some tears), adventures, follies of youth and a loving remembrance. Most of all, they're about holding onto those happy memories with a heart full of love. I hope that this book of memories—some blurry and some as clear as day—gives you a chance to reflect on and remember the most cherished times of your life.

Ruskin Bond

IN GRANDFATHER'S GARDEN

Though the house and grounds of our home in Dehra were Grandfather's domain—where he kept an odd assortment of pets—the magnificent old banyan tree was mine, chiefly because Grandfather, at the age of sixty-five, could no longer climb it. Grandmother used to tease him about this, and would speak of a certain Countess of Desmond, an Englishwoman who lived to the age of 117, and would have lived longer if she hadn't fallen while climbing an apple tree. The spreading branches of the banyan tree, which curved to the ground and took root again, forming a maze of arches, gave me endless pleasure. The tree was older than the house, older than Grandfather, as old as the town of Dehra, nestling in a valley at the foot of the Himalayas.

My first friend and familiar was a small grey squirrel. Arching his back and sniffing into the air, he seemed at first to resent my invasion of his privacy. But when he found that I did not arm myself with a catapult or air-gun, he became friendlier. And when I started leaving him pieces of cake and biscuit, he grew bolder and finally became familiar enough to take food from my hands.

Before long he was delving into my pockets and helping himself to whatever he could find. He was a very young squirrel, and his friends and relatives probably thought him headstrong and foolish for trusting a human.

In the spring, when the banyan tree was full of small red figs, birds of all kinds would flock into its branches, the red-bottomed bulbul, cheerful and greedy; gossiping rosy-pastors; and parrots and crows, squabbling with each other all the time. During the fig season, the banyan tree was the noisiest place on the road.

Halfway up the tree I had built a small platform on which I would often spend the afternoons when it wasn't too hot. I could read there, propping myself up against the bole of the tree with the cushions taken from the drawing room. *Treasure Island*, Huck Finn, the Mowgli stories and detective novels made up my bag of very mixed reading.

When I didn't want to read, I could look down through the banyan leaves at the world below, at Grandmother hanging up or taking down the washing, at the cook quarrelling with a fruit vendor or at Grandfather grumbling at the hardy Indian marigold, which insisted on springing up all over his very English garden. Usually nothing very exciting happened while I was in the banyan tree, but on one particular afternoon I had enough excitement to last me through the summer.

That was the time I saw a mongoose and a cobra fight to death in the garden, while I sat directly above them in the banyan tree.

It was an April afternoon. The warm breezes of approaching summer had sent everyone, including Grandfather, indoors. I was feeling drowsy myself and was wondering if I should go to the pond behind the house for a swim, when I saw a huge black cobra gliding out of a clump of cacti and making for some cooler part of the garden. At the same time a mongoose (whom I had often seen) emerged from the bushes and went straight for the cobra.

In a clearing beneath the tree, in bright sunshine, they came face to face.

The cobra knew only too well that the grey mongoose, three feet long, was a superb fighter, and was clever and aggressive. But the cobra was a skilful and experienced fighter, too. He could move swiftly and strike at the speed of light, and the sacs behind his long, sharp fangs were full of deadly venom.

It was to be a battle of champions.

Hissing defiance, his forked tongue darting in and out, the cobra raised three of his six feet off the ground, and spread his broad, spectacled hood. The mongoose bushed his tail. The long hair on his spine stood up (in the past, the very thickness of his hair had saved him from bites that would have been fatal to others).

Though the combatants were unaware of my presence in the banyan tree, they soon became aware of the arrival of two other spectators. One was a mynah, and the other a jungle crow (not the wily urban crow). They had seen these preparations for battle, and had settled on the cactus to watch the outcome. Had they been content only to watch, all would have been well with both of them.

The cobra stood on the defensive, swaying slowly from side to side, trying to mesmerize the mongoose into making a false move. The mongoose knew the power of his opponent's glassy, twinkling eyes, and refused to meet them. Instead, he fixed his gaze at a point just below the cobra's hood, and opened the attack.

Moving forward quickly until he was just within the cobra's reach, he made a feint to one side. Immediately the cobra struck. His great hood came down so swiftly that I thought nothing could save the mongoose. But the little fellow jumped neatly to one side, and darted in as swiftly as the cobra, biting the snake on the back and darting away again out of reach.

The moment the cobra struck, the crow and the mynah hurled themselves at him, only to collide heavily in mid-air. Shrieking at each other, they returned to the cactus plant.

A few drops of blood glistened on the cobra's back.

The cobra struck again and missed. Again the mongoose sprang aside, jumped in and bit. Again the birds dived at the snake, bumped into each other instead, and returned shrieking to the safety of the cactus.

The third round followed the same course as the first but with one dramatic difference. The crow and the mynah, still determined to take part in the proceedings, dived at the cobra, but this time they missed each other as well as their mark. The mynah flew on and reached its perch, but the crow tried to pull up in mid-air and turn back. In the second that it took him to do this, the cobra whipped his head back and struck with great force, his snout thudding against the crow's body.

I saw the bird flung nearly twenty feet across the garden, where, after fluttering about for a while, it lay still. The mynah remained on the cactus plant, and when the snake and the mongoose returned to the fray it very wisely refrained from interfering again!

The cobra was weakening and the mongoose, walking fearlessly up to it, raised himself on his short legs, and with a lightning snap had the big snake by the snout. The cobra writhed and lashed about in a frightening manner, and even coiled itself about the mongoose, but all to no avail. The little fellow hung grimly on, until the snake had ceased to struggle. He then smeared along its quivering length, gripping it round the hood, and dragging it into the bushes.

The mynah dropped cautiously to the ground, hopped about, peered into the bushes from a safe distance, and then, with a shrill cry of congratulation, flew away.

When I had also made a cautious descent from the tree and returned to the house, I told Grandfather of the fight I had seen. He was pleased that the mongoose had won. He had encouraged it to live in the garden, to keep away the snakes, and fed it regularly with scraps from the kitchen. He had never tried taming it, because a wild mongoose was more useful than a domesticated one.

From the banyan tree I often saw the mongoose patrolling the four corners of the garden, and once I saw him with an egg in his mouth and knew he had been in the poultry house; but he hadn't harmed the birds, and I knew Grandmother would forgive him for stealing as long as he kept the snakes away.

The banyan tree was also the setting for what we were to call the Strange Case of the Grey Squirrel and the White Rat.

The white rat was Grandfather's—he had bought it from the bazaar for four annas—but I would often take it with me into the banyan tree, where it soon struck up a friendship with one of the squirrels. They would go off together on little excursions among the roots and branches of the old tree.

Then the squirrel started building a nest. At first she tried building it in my pockets, and when I went indoors and changed my clothes I would find straw and grass falling out. Then one day Grandmother's knitting was missing. We hunted for it everywhere but without success.

Next day I saw something glinting in the hole in the banyan tree and, going up to investigate, saw that it was the end of Grandmother's steel knitting needle. On looking further, I discovered that the hole was crammed with knitting.

And amongst the wool were three baby squirrels—all of them white!

Grandfather had never seen white squirrels before, and we gazed at them in wonder. We were puzzled for some time, but when I mentioned the white rat's frequent visits to the tree, Grandfather told me that the rat must be the father. Rats and squirrels were related to each other, he said, and so it was quite possible for them to have offspring—in this case, white squirrels!

THE ROOM OF MANY COLOURS

Last week I wrote a story, and all the time I was writing it I thought it was a good story; but when it was finished and I had read it through, I found that there was something missing, that it didn't ring true. So I tore it up. I wrote a poem, about an old man sleeping in the sun, and this was true, but it was finished quickly, and once again I was left with the problem of what to write next. And I remembered my father, who taught me to write; and I thought, why not write about my father, and about the trees we planted, and about the people I knew while growing up and about what happened on the way to growing up…

And so, like Alice, I must begin at the beginning. In the beginning there was this red insect, just like a velvet button, which I found on the front lawn of the bungalow. The grass was still wet with overnight rain.

I placed the insect on the palm of my hand and took it into the house to show my father.

'Look, Dad,' I said, 'I haven't seen an insect like this before. Where has it come from?'

'Where did you find it?' he asked.

'On the grass.'

'It must have come down from the sky,' he said. 'It must have come down with the rain.'

Later he told me how the insect really happened but I preferred his first explanation. It was more fun to have it dropping from the sky.

I was seven at the time, and my father was thirty-seven, but, right from the beginning, he made me feel that I was old enough to talk to him about everything—insects, people, trees, steam engines, King George, comics, crocodiles, the Mahatma, the Viceroy, America, Mozambique and Timbuctoo. We took long walks together, explored old ruins, chased butterflies and waved to passing trains.

My mother had gone away when I was four, and I had very dim memories of her. Most other children had their mothers with them, and I found it a bit strange that mine couldn't stay. Whenever I asked my father why she'd gone, he'd say, 'You'll understand when you grow up.' And if I asked him *where* she had gone, he'd look troubled and say, 'I really don't know.' This was the only question of mine to which he didn't have an answer.

But I was quite happy living alone with my father; I had never known any other kind of life.

We were sitting on an old wall, looking out to sea at a couple of Arab dhows and a tram steamer, when my father said, 'Would you like to go to sea one day?'

'Where does the sea go?' I asked.

'It goes everywhere.'

'Does it go to the end of the world?'

'It goes right round the world. It's a round world.'

'It can't be.'

'It is. But it's so big, you can't see the roundness. When a fly sits on a watermelon, it can't see right round the melon, can it? The melon must seem quite flat to the fly. Well, in comparison to the world, we're much, much smaller than the tiniest of insects.'

'Have you been around the world?' I asked.

'No, only as far as England. That's where your grandfather was born.'

'And my grandmother?'

'She came to India from Norway when she was quite small. Norway is a cold land, with mountains and snow, and the sea cutting deep into the land. I was there as a boy. It's very beautiful, and the people are good and work hard.'

'I'd like to go there.'

'You will, one day. When you are older, I'll take you to Norway.'

'Is it better than England?'

'It's quite different.'

'Is it better than India?'

'It's quite different.'

'Is India like England?'

'No, it's different.'

'Well, what does "different" mean?'

'It means things are not the same. It means people are different. It means the weather is different. It means tree and birds and insects are different.'

'Are English crocodiles different from Indian crocodiles?'

'They don't have crocodiles in England.'

'Oh, then it must be different.'

'It would be a dull world if it was the same everywhere,' said my father.

He never lost patience with my endless questioning. If he wanted a rest, he would take out his pipe and spend a long time lighting it. If this took very long I'd find something else to do.

But sometimes I'd wait patiently until the pipe was drawing, and then return to the attack.

'Will we always be in India?' I asked.

'No, we'll have to go away one day. You see, it's hard to explain, but it isn't really our country.'

'Ayah says it belongs to the king of England, and the jewels in his crown were taken from India, and that when the Indians get their jewels back the king will lose India! But first they have to get the crown from the king, but this is very difficult, she says, because the crown is always on his head. He even sleeps wearing his crown!'

Ayah was my nanny. She loved me deeply, and was always filling my head with strange and wonderful stories.

My father did not comment on Ayah's views. All he said was, 'We'll have to go away some day.'

'How long have we been here?' I asked.

'Two hundred years.'

'No, I mean us.'

'Well, you were born in India, so that's seven years for you.'

'Then can't I stay here?'

'Do you want to?'

'I want to go across the sea. But can we take Ayah with us?'

'I don't know, son. Let's walk along the beach.'

We lived in an old palace beside a lake. The palace looked like a ruin from the outside, but the rooms were cool and comfortable. We lived in one wing, and my father organized a small school in another wing. His pupils were the children of the raja and the raja's relatives. My father had started life in India as a tea planter, but he had been trained as a teacher and the idea of starting a school in a small state facing the Arabian Sea had appealed to him. The pay wasn't much, but we had a palace to live in, the latest 1938 model Hillman to drive about in and a number of servants. In those days, of course, everyone had servants (although the servants did not have any!). Ayah was our own; but the cook, the bearer, the gardener and the bhisti were all provided by the state.

Sometimes I sat in the schoolroom with the other children (who were all much bigger than me), sometimes I remained in the house with Ayah, sometimes I followed the gardener, Dukhi, about the spacious garden.

Dukhi means 'sad', and though I never could discover if the gardener had anything to feel sad about, the name certainly suited him. He had grown to resemble the drooping weeds that he was always digging up with a tiny spade. I seldom saw him standing up. He always sat on the ground with his knees well up to his chin, and attacked the weeds from this position. He could spend all day on his haunches, moving about the garden simply by shuffling his feet along the grass.

I tried to imitate his posture, sitting down on my heels and putting my knees into my armpits, but I could never hold the position for more than five minutes.

Time had no meaning in a large garden, and Dukhi never hurried. Life, for him, was not a matter of one year succeeding another, but of five seasons—winter, spring, hot weather, monsoon and autumn—arriving and departing. His seedbeds always had to be in readiness for the coming season, and he did not look any further than the next monsoon. It was impossible to tell his age. He may have been thirty-six or eighty-six. He was either very young for his years or very old for them.

Dukhi loved bright colours, especially reds and yellows. He liked strongly scented flowers, like jasmine and honeysuckle. He couldn't understand my father's preference for the more delicately perfumed petunias and sweetpeas. But I shared Dukhi's fondness for the common bright orange marigold, which is offered in temples and is used to make garlands and nosegays. When the garden was bare of all colour, the marigold would still be there, gay and flashy, challenging the sun.

Dukhi was very fond of making nosegays, and I liked to watch him at work. A sunflower formed the centrepiece. It was surrounded by roses, marigolds and oleander, fringed with green leaves and bound together with silver thread. The perfume was overpowering. The nosegays were presented to me or my father on special occasions, that is, on a birthday or to guests of my father's who were considered important.

One day I found Dukhi making a nosegay, and said, 'No one is coming today, Dukhi. It isn't even a birthday.'

'It is a birthday, Chota Sahib,' he said. 'Chota Sahib' was the title he had given me. It wasn't much of a title compared to Raja Sahib, Diwan Sahib or Burra Sahib, but it was nice to have a title at the age of seven.

'Oh,' I said. 'And is there a party, too?'

'No party.'

'What's the use of a birthday without a party? What's the use of a birthday without presents?'

'This person doesn't like presents—just flowers.'

'Who is it?' I asked, full of curiosity.

'If you want to find out, you can take these flowers to her. She lives right at the top of that far side of the palace. There are twenty-two steps to climb. Remember that, Chota Sahib, you take twenty-three steps and you will go over the edge and into the lake!'

I started climbing the stairs.

It was a spiral staircase of wrought iron, and it went round and round and up and up, and it made me quite dizzy and tired.

At the top I found myself on a small balcony, which looked out over the lake and another palace, at the crowded city and the distant harbour. I heard a voice, a rather high, musical voice, saying (in English), 'Are you a ghost?' I turned to see who had spoken but found the balcony empty. The voice had come from a dark room.

I turned to the stairway, ready to flee, but the voice said, 'Oh, don't go, there's nothing to be frightened of!'

And so I stood still, peering cautiously into the darkness of the room.

'First, tell me—are you a ghost?'

'I'm a boy,' I said.

'And I'm a girl. We can be friends. I can't come out there, so you had better come in. Come along, I'm not a ghost either—not yet, anyway!'

As there was nothing very frightening about the voice, I stepped into the room. It was dark inside, and coming in from the glare, it took me some time to make out the tiny, elderly lady seated on a cushioned gilt chair. She wore a red sari, lots of coloured bangles on her wrists and golden earrings. Her hair was streaked with white, but her skin was still quite smooth and unlined, and she had large and very beautiful eyes.

'You must be Master Bond!' she said. 'Do you know who I am?'

'You're a lady with a birthday,' I said, 'but that's all I know. Dukhi didn't tell me any more.'

'If you promise to keep it a secret, I'll tell you who I am. You see, everyone thinks I'm mad. Do you think so too?'

'I don't know.'

'Well, you must tell me if you think so,' she said with a

chuckle. Her laugh was the sort of sound made by the gecko, a little wall lizard, coming from deep down in the throat. 'I have a feeling you are a truthful boy. Do you find it very difficult to tell the truth?'

'Sometimes.'

'Sometimes. Of course, there are times when I tell lies—lots of little lies—because they're such fun! But would you call me a liar? I wouldn't, if I were you, but would *you*?'

'Are you a liar?'

'I'm asking you! If I were to tell you that I was a queen—that I *am* a queen—would you believe me?'

I thought deeply about this, and then said, 'I'll try to believe you.'

'Oh, but you *must* believe me. I'm a real queen, I'm a rani! Look, I've got diamonds to prove it!' And she held out her hands and there was a ring on each finger, the stones glowing and glittering in the dim light. 'Diamonds, rubies, pearls and emeralds! Only a queen can have these!' She was most anxious that I should believe her.

'You must be a queen,' I said.

'Right!' she snapped. 'In that case, would you mind calling me "Your Highness"?'

'Your Highness,' I said.

She smiled. It was a slow, beautiful smile. Her whole face lit up.

'I could love you,' she said. 'But better still, I'll give you something to eat. Do you like chocolates?'

'Yes, Your Highness.'

'Well,' she said, taking a box from the table beside her, 'these have come all the way from England. Take two. Only two, mind, otherwise the box will finish before Thursday, and

I don't want that to happen because I won't get any more till Saturday. That's when Captain MacWhirr's ship gets in, the *SS Lucy*, loaded with boxes and boxes of chocolates!'

'All for you?' I asked in considerable awe.

'Yes, of course. They have to last at least three months. I get them from England. I get only the best chocolates. I like them with pink crunchy fillings, don't you?'

'Oh, yes!' I exclaimed, full of envy.

'Never mind,' she said, 'I may give you one, now and then—if you're very nice to me! Here you are, help yourself...' She pushed the chocolate box towards me.

I took a silver-wrapped chocolate, and then just as I was thinking of taking a second, she quickly took the box away.

'No more!' she said. 'They have to last till Saturday.'

'But I took only *one*,' I said with some indignation.

'Did you?' She gave me a sharp look, decided I was telling the truth, and said graciously, 'Well, in that case you can have another.'

Watching the rani carefully, in case she snatched the box away again, I selected a second chocolate, this one with a green wrapper. I don't remember what kind of day it was outside, but I remember the bright green of the chocolate wrapper.

I thought it would be rude to eat the chocolates in front of a queen, so I put them in my pocket and said, 'I'd better go now. Ayah will be looking for me.'

'And when will you be coming to see me again?'

'I don't know,' I said.

'There's something I want you to do for me,' she said, placing one finger on my shoulder and giving me a conspiratorial look. 'Will you do it?'

'What is it, Your Highness?'

'What is it? Why do you ask? A real prince never asks where or why or whatever, he simply does what the princess asks of him. When I was a princess—before I became a queen, that is—I asked a prince to swim across the lake and fetch me a lily growing on the other bank.'

'And did he get it for you?'

'He drowned halfway across. Let that be a lesson to you. Never agree to do something without knowing what it is.'

'But I thought you said...'

'Never mind what I said. It's what I say that matters!'

'Oh, all right,' I said, fidgeting to be gone. 'What is it you want me to do?'

'Nothing.' Her tiny rosebud lips pouted and she stared sullenly at a picture on the wall. Now that my eyes had grown used to the dim light in the room, I noticed that the walls were hung with portraits of stout rajas and ranis, turbaned and bedecked in fine clothes. There were also portraits of Queen Victoria and King George V of England. And, in the centre of all this distinguished company, a large picture of Mickey Mouse.

'I'll do it if it isn't too dangerous,' I said.

'Then listen.' She took my hand and drew me towards her—what a tiny hand she had!—and whispered, 'I want a *red* rose from the palace garden. But be careful! Don't let Dukhi the gardener catch you. He'll know it's for me. He knows I love roses. And he hates me! I'll tell you why, one day. But if he catches you, he'll do something terrible.'

'To me?'

'No, to himself. That's much worse, isn't it? He'll tie himself into knots, or lie naked on a bed of thorns, or go on a long fast with nothing to eat but fruit, sweets and chicken! So you will be careful, won't you?'

'Oh, but he doesn't hate you,' I cried in protest, remembering the flowers he'd sent for her, and looking around I found that I'd been sitting on them. 'Look, he sent these flowers for your birthday!'

'Well, if he sent them for my birthday, you can take them back,' she snapped. 'But if he sent them for *me*...' and she suddenly softened and looked coy, 'then I might keep them. Thank you, my dear, it was a very sweet thought.' And she leaned forward as though to kiss me.

'It's late, I must go!' I said in alarm and, turning on my heels, ran out of the room and down the spiral staircase.

Father hadn't started lunch, or rather tiffin, as we called it then. He usually waited for me if I was late. I don't suppose he enjoyed eating alone.

For tiffin we usually had rice, mutton curry (koftas or meat balls, with plenty of gravy, was my favourite curry), fried dal and a hot lime or mango pickle. For supper, we had English food—a soup, roast pork and fried potatoes, a rich gravy made by my father and a custard or caramel pudding. My father enjoyed cooking, but it was only in the morning that he found time for it. Breakfast was his own creation. He cooked eggs in a variety of interesting ways, and favoured some Italian recipes which he had collected during a trip to Europe, long before I was born.

In deference to the feelings of our Hindu friends, we did not eat beef, but, apart from mutton and chicken, there was a plentiful supply of other meats—partridge, venison, lobster and even porcupine!

'And where have you been?' asked my father, helping himself to rice as soon as he saw me come in.

'To the top of the old palace,' I said.

'Did you meet anyone there?'

'Yes, I met a tiny lady who told me she was a rani. She gave me chocolates.'

'As a rule, she doesn't like visitors.'

'Oh, she didn't mind me. But is she really a queen?'

'Well, she's the daughter of a maharaja. That makes her a princess. She never married. There's a story that she fell in love with a commoner, one of the palace servants, and wanted to marry him, but of course they wouldn't allow that. She became very melancholic, and started living all by herself in the old palace. They give her everything she needs, but she doesn't go out or have visitors. Everyone says she's mad.'

'How do they know?' I asked.

'Because she's different from other people, I suppose.'

'Is that being mad?'

'No. Not really, I suppose madness is not seeing things as others see them.'

'Is that very bad?'

'No,' said Father, who for once was finding it very difficult to explain something to me. 'But people who are like that—people whose minds are so different that they don't think, step by step, as we do, whose thoughts jump all over the place—such people are very difficult to live with...'

'Step by step,' I repeated. 'Step by step...'

'You aren't eating,' said my father. 'Hurry up, and you can come with me to school today.'

I always looked forward to attending my father's classes. He did not take me to the schoolroom very often, because he wanted school to be a treat, to begin with, and then later the routine wouldn't be so unwelcome.

Sitting there with older children, understanding only half

of what they were learning, I felt important and part grown-up. And of course I did learn to read and write, although I first learnt to read upside-down, by means of standing in front of the others' desks and peering across at their books. Later, when I went to school, I had some difficulty in learning to read the right way up; and even today I sometimes read upside-down, for the sake of variety. I don't mean that I read standing on my head, simply that I held the book upside-down.

I had at my command a number of rhymes and jingles, the most interesting of these being 'Solomon Grundy'.

Solomon Grundy,
Born on a Monday,
Christened on Tuesday,
Married on Wednesday,
Took ill on Thursday,
Worse on Friday,
Died on Saturday,
Buried on Sunday:
This is the end of
Solomon Grundy.

Was that all that life amounted to, in the end? And were we all Solomon Grundys? These were questions that bothered me at the time. Another puzzling rhyme was the one that went:

Hark, hark,
The dogs do bark,
The beggars are coming to town;
Some in rags,
Some in bags,
And some in velvet gowns.

This rhyme puzzled me for a long time. There were beggars aplenty in the bazaar, and sometimes they came to the house, and some of them did wear rags and bags (and some nothing at all) and the dogs did bark at them, but the beggar in the velvet gown never came our way.

'Who's this beggar in a velvet gown?'

I asked my father. 'Not a beggar at all,' he said.

'Then why call him one?'

And I went to Ayah and asked her the same question, 'Who is the beggar in the velvet gown?'

'Jesus Christ,' said Ayah.

Ayah was a fervent Christian and made me say my prayers at night, even when I was very sleepy. She had, I think, Arab and Negro blood in addition to the blood of the Koli fishing community to which her mother had belonged. Her father, a sailor on an Arab dhow, had been a convert to Christianity. Ayah was a large, buxom woman, with heavy hands and feet and a slow, swaying gait that had all the grace and majesty of a royal elephant. Elephants for all their size are nimble creatures; and Ayah, too, was nimble, sensitive and gentle with her big hands. Her face was always sweet and childlike.

Although a Christian, she clung to many of the beliefs of her parents and loved to tell me stories about mischievous spirits and evil spirits, humans who changed into animals, and snakes who had been princes in their former lives.

There was the story of the snake who married a princess. At first the princess did not wish to marry the snake, whom she had met in a forest, but the snake insisted saying, 'I'll kill you if you won't marry me,' and of course that settled the question. The snake led his bride away and took her to a great treasure. 'I was a prince in my former life,' he explained. 'This treasure is yours.' And then the snake very gallantly disappeared.

'Snakes,' declared Ayah, 'were very lucky omens if seen early in the morning.'

'But, what if the snake bites the lucky person?' I asked.

'He will be lucky all the same,' said Ayah with a logic that was all her own.

Snakes! There were a number of them living in the big garden, and my father had advised me to avoid the long grass. But I had seen snakes crossing the road (a lucky omen, according to Ayah) and they were never aggressive.

'A snake won't attack you,' said Father, 'provided you leave it alone. Of course, if you step on one it will probably bite.'

'Are all snakes poisonous?'

'Yes, but only a few are poisonous enough to kill a man. Others use their poison on rats and frogs. A good thing, too, otherwise during the rains the house would be taken over by the frogs.'

One afternoon, while Father was at school, Ayah found a snake in the bathtub. It wasn't early morning and so the snake couldn't have been a lucky one. Ayah was frightened and ran into the garden calling for help. Dukhi came running. Ayah ordered me to stay outside while they went after the snake.

And it was while I was alone in the garden—an unusual circumstance, since Dukhi was nearly always there—that I remembered the rani's request. On an impulse, I went to the nearest rose bush and plucked the largest rose, pricking my thumb in the process.

And then, without waiting to see what had happened to the snake (it finally escaped), I started up the steps to the top of the old palace.

When I got to the top, I knocked on the door of the rani's

room. Getting no reply, I walked along the balcony until I reached another doorway. There were wooden panels around the door, with elephants, camels and turbaned warriors carved into it. As the door was open, I walked boldly into the room then stood still in astonishment. The room was filled with a strange light.

There were windows going right round the room, and each small windowpane was made of a different coloured glass. The sun that came through one window flung red and green and purple colours on the figure of the little rani who stood there with her face pressed to the glass.

She spoke to me without turning from the window. 'This is my favourite room. I have all the colours here. I can see a different world through each pane of glass. Come, join me!' And she beckoned to me, her small hand fluttering like a delicate butterfly.

I went up to the rani. She was only a little taller than me, and we were able to share the same windowpane.

'See, it's a red world!' she said.

The garden below, the palace and the lake were all tinted red. I watched the rani's world for a little while and then touched her on the arm and said, 'I have brought you a rose!'

She started away from me, and her eyes looked frightened. She would not look at the rose.

'Oh, why did you bring it?' she cried, wringing her hands. 'He'll be arrested now!'

'Who'll be arrested?'

'The prince, of course!'

'But *I* took it,' I said. 'No one saw me. Ayah and Dukhi were inside the house, catching a snake.'

'Did they catch it?' she asked, forgetting about the rose.

'I don't know. I didn't wait to see!'

'They should follow the snake, instead of catching it. It may lead them to a treasure. All snakes have treasures to guard.'

This seemed to confirm what Ayah had been telling me, and I resolved that I would follow the next snake that I met.

'Don't you like the rose, then?' I asked.

'Did you steal it?'

'Yes.'

'Good. Flowers should always be stolen. They're more fragrant then.'

Because of a man called Hitler, war had been declared in Europe and Britain was fighting Germany.

In my comic papers, the Germans were usually shown as blundering idiots; so I didn't see how Britain could possibly lose the War, nor why it should concern India, nor why it should be necessary for my father to join up. But I remember him showing me a newspaper headline which said:

BOMBS FALL ON BUCKINGHAM PALACE—
KING AND QUEEN SAFE

I expect that had something to do with it.

He went to Delhi for an interview with the RAF and I was left in Ayah's charge.

It was a week I remember well, because it was the first time I had been left on my own. That first night I was afraid—afraid of the dark, afraid of the emptiness of the house, afraid of the howling of the jackals outside. The loud ticking of the clock was the only reassuring sound: clocks really made themselves heard in those days! I tried concentrating on the ticking, shutting out other sounds and the menace of the dark, but it wouldn't work. I thought I heard a faint hissing near the bed, and sat up, bathed in perspiration, certain that a snake was in the room. I shouted for Ayah and she came running, switching on all the lights.

'A snake!' I cried. 'There's a snake in the room!'

'Where, baba?'

'I don't know where, but I *heard* it.'

Ayah looked under the bed, and behind the chairs and tables, but there was no snake to be found. She persuaded me that I must have heard the breeze whispering in the mosquito curtains.

But I didn't want to be left alone.

'I'm coming to you,' I said and followed her into her small room near the kitchen.

Ayah slept on a low string cot. The mattress was thin, the blanket worn and patched up; but Ayah's warm and solid body made up for the discomfort of the bed. I snuggled up to her and was soon asleep.

I had almost forgotten the rani in the old palace and was about to pay her a visit when, to my surprise, I found her in the garden. I had risen early that morning, and had gone running barefoot over the dew-drenched grass. No one was about, but I startled a flock of parrots and the birds rose screeching from a banyan tree and wheeled away to some other corner of the palace grounds. I was just in time to see a mongoose scurrying across the grass with an egg in its mouth. The mongoose must have been raiding the poultry farm at the palace.

I was trying to locate the mongoose's hideout, and was on all fours in a jungle of tall cosmos plants when I heard the rustle of clothes, and turned to find the rani staring at me.

She didn't ask me what I was doing there, but simply said: 'I don't think he could have gone in there.'

'But I saw him go this way,' I said.

'Nonsense! He doesn't live in this part of the garden. He lives in the roots of the banyan tree.'

'But that's where the snake lives,' I said.

'You mean the snake who was a prince. Well, that's whom I'm looking for!'

'A snake who was a prince!' I gaped at the rani.

She made a gesture of impatience with her butterfly hands, and said, 'Tut, you're only a child, you can't understand. The prince lives in the roots of the banyan tree, but he comes out early every morning. Have you seen him?'

'No. But I saw a mongoose.'

The rani became frightened. 'Oh dear, is there a mongoose in the garden? He might kill the prince!'

'How can a mongoose kill a prince?' I asked.

'You don't understand, Master Bond. Princes, when they die, are born again as snakes.'

'*All* princes?'

'No, only those who die before they can marry.'

'Did your prince die before he could marry you?'

'Yes. And he returned to this garden in the form of a beautiful snake.'

'Well,' I said, 'I hope it wasn't the snake the water carrier killed last week.'

'He killed a snake!' The rani looked horrified. She was quivering all over. 'It might have been the prince!'

'It was a brown snake,' I said.

'Oh, then it wasn't him.' She looked very relieved. 'Brown snakes are only ministers and people like that. It has to be a green snake to be a prince.'

'I haven't seen any green snakes here.'

'There's one living in the roots of the banyan tree. You won't kill it, will you?'

'Not if it's really a prince.'

'And you won't let others kill it?'

'I'll tell Ayah.'

'Good. You're on my side. But be careful of the gardener. Keep him away from the banyan tree. He's always killing snakes. I don't trust him at all.'

She came nearer and, leaning forward a little, looked into my eyes.

'Blue eyes—I trust them. But don't trust green eyes. And yellow eyes are evil.'

'I've never seen yellow eyes.'

'That's because you're pure,' she said and turned away and hurried across the lawn as though she had just remembered a very urgent appointment.

The sun was up, slanting through the branches of the banyan tree, and Ayah's voice could be heard calling me for breakfast.

'Dukhi,' I said, when I found him in the garden later that day, 'don't kill the snake in the banyan tree.'

'A snake in the banyan tree!' he exclaimed, seizing his hose.

'No, no!' I said. 'I haven't seen it. But the rani says there's one. She says it was a prince in its former life, and that we shouldn't kill it.'

'Oh,' said Dukhi, smiling to himself. 'The rani says so. All right, you tell her we won't kill it.'

'Is it true that she was in love with a prince but that he died before she could marry him?'

'Something like that,' said Dukhi. 'It was a long time ago—before I came here.'

'My father says it wasn't a prince, but a commoner. Are you a commoner, Dukhi?'

'A commoner? What's that, Chota Sahib?'

'I'm not sure. Someone very poor, I suppose.'

'Then I must be a commoner,' said Dukhi.

'Were you in love with the rani?' I asked.

Dukhi was so startled that he dropped his hose and lost his balance; the first time I'd seen him lose his poise while squatting on his haunches.

'Don't say such things, Chota Sahib!'

'Why not?'

'You'll get me into trouble.'

'Then it must be true.'

Dukhi threw up his hands in mock despair and started collecting his implements.

'It's true, it's true!' I cried, dancing round him, and then I ran indoors to Ayah and said, 'Ayah, Dukhi was in love with the rani!'

Ayah gave a shriek of laughter, then looked very serious and put her finger against my lips.

'Don't say such things,' she said. 'Dukhi is of a very low caste. People won't like it if they hear what you say. And besides, the rani told you her prince died and turned into a snake. Well, Dukhi hasn't become a snake as yet, has he?'

True, Dukhi didn't look as though he could be anything but a gardener; but I wasn't satisfied with his denials or with Ayah's attempts to still my tongue. Hadn't Dukhi sent the rani a nosegay?

When my father came home, he looked quite pleased with himself.

'What have you brought for me?' was the first question I asked.

He had brought me some new books, a dartboard and a train set; and in my excitement over examining these gifts, I forgot to ask about the result of his trip.

It was during tiffin that he told me what had happened—and what was going to happen.

'We'll be going away soon,' he said. 'I've joined the Royal Air Force. I'll have to work in Delhi.'

'Oh! Will you be in the War, Dad? Will you fly a plane?'

'No, I'm too old to be flying planes. I'll be forty years old in July. The RAF will be giving me what they call intelligence work—decoding secret messages and things like that and I don't suppose I'll be able to tell you much about it.'

This didn't sound as exciting as flying planes, but it sounded important and rather mysterious.

'Well, I hope it's interesting,' I said. 'Is Delhi a good place to live in?'

'I'm not sure. It will be very hot by the middle of April. And you won't be able to stay with me, Ruskin—not at first, anyway, not until I can get married quarters and then, only if your mother returns... Meanwhile, you'll stay with your grandmother in Dehra.' He must have seen the disappointment in my face, because he quickly added: 'Of course, I'll come to see you often. Dehra isn't far from Delhi—only a night's train journey.'

But I was dismayed. It wasn't that I didn't want to stay with my grandmother, but I had grown so used to sharing my father's life and even watching him at work, that the thought of being separated from him was unbearable.

'Not as bad as going to boarding school,' he said. 'And that's the only alternative.'

'Not boarding school,' I said quickly, 'I'll run away from boarding school.'

'Well, you won't want to run away from your grandmother. She's very fond of you. And if you come with me to Delhi, you'll be alone all day in a stuffy little hut while I'm away at work.

Sometimes I may have to go on tour—then what happens?'

'I don't mind being on my own.' And this was true. I had already grown accustomed to having my own room and my own trunk and my own bookshelf and I felt as though I was about to lose these things.

'Will Ayah come too?' I asked.

My father looked thoughtful. 'Would you like that?'

'Ayah must come,' I said firmly. 'Otherwise I'll run away.'

'I'll have to ask her,' said my father.

Ayah, it turned out, was quite ready to come with us. In fact, she was indignant that Father should have considered leaving her behind. She had brought me up since my mother went away, and she wasn't going to hand over charge to any upstart aunt or governess. She was pleased and excited at the prospect of the move, and this helped to raise my spirits.

'What is Dehra like?' I asked my father.

'It's a green place,' he said. 'It lies in a valley in the foothills of the Himalayas and it's surrounded by forests. There are lots of trees in Dehra.'

'Does Grandmother's house have trees?'

'Yes. There's a big jackfruit tree in the garden. Your grandmother planted it when I was a boy. And there's an old banyan tree, which is good to climb. And there are fruit trees, litchis, mangoes, papayas.'

'Are there any books?'

'Grandmother's books won't interest you. But I'll be bringing you books from Delhi whenever I come to see you.'

I was beginning to look forward to the move. Changing houses had always been fun. Changing towns ought to be fun, too.

A few days before we left, I went to say goodbye to the rani.

'I'm going away,' I said.

'How lovely!' said the rani. 'I wish I could go away!'

'Why don't you?'

'They won't let me. They're afraid to let me out of the palace.'

'What are they afraid of, Your Highness?'

'That I might run away. Run away, far, far away, to the land where the leopards are learning to pray.'

Gosh, I thought, she's really quite crazy... But then she was silent, and started smoking a small hookah.

She drew on the hookah, looked at me, and asked, 'Where is your mother?'

'I haven't one.'

'Everyone has a mother. Did yours die?'

'No. She went away.'

She drew on her hookah again and then said, very sweetly, 'Don't go away...'

'I must,' I said. 'It's because of the War.'

'What war? Is there a war on? You see, no one tells me anything.'

'It's between us and Hitler,' I said.

'And who is Hitler?'

'He's a German.'

'I knew a German once, Dr Schreinherr, he had beautiful hands.'

'Was he an artist?'

'He was a dentist.'

The rani got up from her couch and accompanied me out on to the balcony. When we looked down at the garden, we could see Dukhi weeding a flower bed. Both of us gazed down at him in silence, and I wondered what the rani would say if I asked her if she had ever been in love with the palace gardener.

Ayah had told me it would be an insulting question, so I held my peace. But as I walked slowly down the spiral staircase, the rani's voice came after me.

'Thank him,' she said. 'Thank him for the beautiful rose.'

THE LAST TONGA RIDE

It was a warm spring day in Dehra, and the walls of the bungalow were aflame with flowering bougainvillaea. The papayas were ripening. The scent of sweetpeas drifted across the garden. Grandmother sat in an easy chair in a shady corner of the verandah, her knitting needles clicking away, her head nodding now and then. She was knitting a pullover for my father. 'Delhi has cold winters,' she had said; and although the winter was still eight months away, she had set to work on getting our woollens ready.

In the Kathiawar states, touched by the warm waters of the Arabian Sea, it had never been cold but Dehra lies at the foot of the first range of the Himalayas.

Grandmother's hair was white, her eyes were not very strong but her fingers moved quickly with the needles and the needles kept clicking all morning.

When Grandmother wasn't looking, I picked geranium leaves, crushed them between my fingers and pressed them to my nose.

I had been in Dehra with my grandmother for almost a month and I had not seen my father during this time. We had never before been separated for so long. He wrote to me every week, and sent me books and picture postcards; and I would walk to the end of the road to meet the postman as early as possible, to see if there was any mail for us.

We heard the jingle of tonga-bells at the gate, and a familiar horse-buggy came rattling up the drive.

'I'll see who's come,' I said, and ran down the verandah steps and across the garden.

It was Bansi Lal in his tonga. There were many tongas and tonga-drivers in Dehra but Bansi was my favourite driver. He was young and handsome and he always wore a clean white shirt and pyjamas. His pony, too, was bigger and faster than the other tonga ponies. Bansi didn't have a passenger, so I asked him, 'What have you come for, Bansi?'

'Your grandmother sent for me, dost.' He did not call me 'chota sahib' or 'baba', but 'dost' and this made me feel much more important. Not every small boy could boast of a tonga-driver for his friend!

'Where are you going, Granny?' I asked, after I had run back to the verandah.

'I'm going to the bank.'

'Can I come too?'

'Whatever for? What will you do in the bank?'

'Oh, I won't come inside, I'll sit in the tonga with Bansi.'

'Come along, then.'

We helped Grandmother into the back seat of the tonga, and then I joined Bansi in the driver's seat. He said something to his pony and the pony set off at a brisk trot, out of the gate and down the road.

'Now, not too fast, Bansi,' said Grandmother, who didn't like anything that went too fast—tonga, motor car, train or bullock-cart.

'Fast?' said Bansi. 'Have no fear, Memsahib. This pony has never gone fast in its life. Even if a bomb went off behind us, we could go no faster. I have another pony, which I use for racing when customers are in a hurry. This pony is reserved for you, Memsahib.'

There was no other pony, but Grandmother did not know this, and was mollified by the assurance that she was riding in the slowest tonga in Dehra.

A ten-minute ride brought us to the bazaar. Grandmother's bank, the Allahabad Bank, stood near the clock tower. She was gone for about half an hour and during this period Bansi and I sauntered about in front of the shops. The pony had been left with some green stuff to munch.

'Do you have any money on you?' asked Bansi.

'Four annas,' I said.

'Just enough for two cups of tea,' said Bansi, putting his arm round my shoulders and guiding me towards a tea stall. The money passed from my palm to his.

'You can have tea, if you like,' I said. 'I'll have a lemonade.'

'So be it, friend. A tea and a lemonade, and be quick about it,' said Bansi to the boy in the stall and presently the drinks were set before us. Bansi was making a sound rather like his pony when he drank, while I burped my way through some green, gaseous stuff that tasted more like soap than lemonade.

When Grandmother came out of the bank, she looked pensive, and did not talk much during the ride back to the house except to tell me to behave myself when I leaned over to pat the pony on its rump. After paying off Bansi, she marched straight indoors.

'When will you come again?' I asked Bansi.

'When my services are required, dost. I have to make a living, you know. But I tell you what, since we are friends, the next time I am passing this way after leaving a fare, I will jingle my bells at the gate and if you are free and would like a ride—a fast ride—you can join me. It won't cost you anything. Just bring some money for a cup of tea.'

'All right—since we are friends,' I said.

'Since we are friends.'

And touching the pony very lightly with the handle of his whip, he sent the tonga rattling up the drive and out of the gate. I could hear Bansi singing as the pony cantered down the road.

Ayah was waiting for me in the bedroom, her hands resting on her broad hips—sure sign of an approaching storm.

'So you went off to the bazaar without telling me,' she said. (It wasn't enough that I had Grandmother's permission!) 'And all this time I've been waiting to give you your bath.'

'It's too late now, isn't it?' I asked hopefully.

'No, it isn't. There's still an hour left for lunch. Off with your clothes!'

While I undressed, Ayah berated me for keeping the company of tonga-drivers like Bansi. I think she was a little jealous.

'He is a rogue, that man. He drinks, gambles and smokes opium. He has TB and other terrible diseases. So don't you be too friendly with him, understand, baba?'

I nodded my head sagely but said nothing. I thought Ayah was exaggerating, as she always did about people, and besides, I had no intention of giving up free tonga rides.

As my father had told me, Dehra was a good place for trees, and Grandmother's house was surrounded by several kinds— peepul, seem, mango, jackfruit, papaya and an ancient banyan tree. Some of the trees had been planted by my father and grandfather.

'How old is the jackfruit tree?' I asked Grandmother.

'Now let me see,' said Grandmother, looking very thoughtful. 'I should remember the jackfruit tree. Oh yes, your grandfather put it down in 1927. It was during the rainy season. I remember, because it was your father's birthday and we celebrated it by planting a tree. 14 July 1927. Long before you were born!'

The banyan tree grew behind the house. Its spreading branches, which hung to the ground and took root again, formed a number of twisting passageways in which I liked to wander. The tree was older than the house, older than my grandparents, as old as Dehra. I could hide myself in its branches behind thick, green leaves and spy on the world below.

It was an enormous tree, about sixty feet high, and the first time I saw it I trembled with excitement because I had never seen such a marvellous tree before. I approached it slowly, even cautiously, as I wasn't sure the tree wanted my friendship. It looked as though it had many secrets. There were sounds and movement in the branches but I couldn't see who or what made the sounds.

The tree made the first move, the first overture of friendship. It allowed a leaf to fall.

The leaf brushed against my face as it floated down, but before it could reach the ground I caught and held it. I studied the leaf, running my fingers over its smooth, glossy texture. Then I put out my hand and touched the rough bark of the tree and this felt good to me. So I removed my shoes and socks as people do when they enter a holy place; and finding first a foothold and then a handhold on that broad trunk, I pulled myself up with the help of the tree's aerial roots.

As I climbed, it seemed as though someone was helping me; invisible hands, the hands of the spirit in the tree, touched me and helped me climb.

But although the tree wanted me, there were others who were disturbed and alarmed by my arrival. A pair of parrots suddenly shot out of a hole in the trunk and, with shrill cries, flew across the garden—flashes of green and red and gold. A squirrel looked out from behind a branch, saw me, and went scurrying away to inform his friends and relatives.

I climbed higher, looked up and saw a red beak poised above my head. I shrank away, but the hornbill made no attempt to attack me. He was relaxing in his home, which was a great hole in the tree trunk. Only the bird's head and great beak were showing. He looked at me in a rather bored way, drowsily opening and shutting his eyes.

'So many creatures live here,' I said to myself. 'I hope none of them are dangerous!'

At that moment, the hornbill lunged at a passing cricket. The hornbill and tree trunk met with a loud and resonant 'Tonk'.

I was so startled that I nearly fell out of the tree. But it was a difficult tree to fall out of! It was full of places where one could sit or even lie down. So I moved away from the hornbill, crawled along a branch that had sent out supports, and so moved quite a distance from the main body of the tree. I left its cold, dark depths for an area penetrated by shafts of sunlight.

No one could see me. I lay flat on the broad branch hidden by a screen of leaves. People passed by on the road below. A sahib in a sun-helmet. His memsahib twirling a coloured silk sun-umbrella. Obviously she did not want to get too brown and be mistaken for a country-born person. Behind them, a pram wheeled along by a nanny.

Then there were a number of Indians; some in white dhotis, some in western clothes, some in loincloths. Some with baskets on their heads. Others with coolies to carry their baskets for them.

A cloud of dust, the blare of a horn and down the road, like an out-of-condition dragon, came the latest Morris touring car. Then cyclists. Then a man with a basket of papayas balanced on his head. Following him, a man with a performing monkey. This man rattled a little hand drum, and children followed the man and the monkey along the road. They stopped in the shade of a mango tree on the other side of the road. The little red monkey wore a frilled dress and a baby's bonnet. It danced for the children, while the man sang and played his drum.

The clip-clop of a tonga pony, and Bansi's tonga came rattling down the road. I called down to him and he reined in with a shout of surprise, and looked up into the branches of the banyan tree.

'What are you doing up there?' he cried.

'Hiding from Grandmother,' I said.

'And when are you coming for that ride?'

'On Tuesday afternoon,' I said.

'Why not today?'

'Ayah won't let me. But she has Tuesdays off.'

Bansi spat red paan juice across the road. 'Your ayah is jealous,' he said.

'I know,' I said. 'Women are always jealous, aren't they? I suppose it's because she doesn't have a tonga.'

'It's because she doesn't have a tonga-driver,' said Bansi, grinning up at me. 'Never mind. I'll come on Tuesday—that's the day after tomorrow, isn't it?'

I nodded down to him, and then started backing along my branch, because I could hear Ayah calling in the distance. Bansi leant forward and smacked his pony across the rump, and the tonga shot forward.

'What were you doing up there?' asked Ayah a little later.

'I was watching a snake cross the road,' I said. I knew she couldn't resist talking about snakes. There weren't as many in Dehra as there had been in Kathiawar and she was thrilled that I had seen one.

'Was it moving towards you or away from you?' she asked.

'It was going away.'

Ayah's face clouded over. 'That means poverty for the beholder,' she said gloomily.

Later, while scrubbing me down in the bathroom, she began to air all her prejudices, which included drunkards ('they die quickly anyway'), misers ('they get murdered sooner or later') and tonga-drivers ('they have all the vices').

'You are a very lucky boy,' she said suddenly, peering closely at my tummy.

'Why?' I asked. 'You just said I would be poor because I saw a snake going the wrong way.'

'Well, you won't be poor for long. You have a mole on your tummy, and that's very lucky. And there is one under your armpit, which means you will be famous. Do you have one on the neck? No, thank God! A mole on the neck is the sign of a murderer!'

'Do you have any moles?' I asked.

Ayah nodded seriously, and pulling her sleeve up to her shoulder, showed me a large mole high on her arm.

'What does that mean?' I asked.

'It means a life of great sadness,' said Ayah gloomily.

'Can I touch it?' I asked.

'Yes, touch it,' she said, and taking my hand, she placed it against the mole.

'It's a nice mole,' I said, wanting to make Ayah happy. 'Can I kiss it?'

'You can kiss it,' said Ayah.

I kissed her on the mole.

'That's nice,' she said.

Tuesday afternoon came at last, and as soon as Grandmother was asleep and Ayah had gone to the bazaar, I was at the gate, looking up and down the road for Bansi and his tonga. He was not long in coming. Before the tonga turned into the road, I could hear his voice, singing to the accompaniment of the carriage bells. He reached down, took my hand and hoisted me on to the seat beside him. Then we went off down the road at a steady jogtrot. It was only when we reached the outskirts of the town that Bansi encouraged his pony to greater efforts. He rose in his seat, leaned forward and slapped the pony across the haunches. From a brisk trot we changed to a carefree canter. The tonga swayed from side to side. I clung to Bansi's free arm, while he grinned at me, his mouth red with paan juice.

'Where shall we go, dost?' he asked.

'Nowhere,' I said. 'Anywhere.'

'We'll go to the river,' said Bansi

The 'river' was really a swift mountain stream that ran through the forests outside Dehra, joining the Ganga about fifteen miles away. It was almost dry during the winter and early summer; in flood during the monsoon.

The road out of Dehra was a gentle decline and soon we were rushing headlong through the tea gardens and eucalyptus forests, the pony's hoofs striking sparks off the metalled road, the carriage wheels groaning and creaking so loudly that I feared one of them would come off and that we would all be thrown into a ditch or into the small canal that ran beside the road. We swept through mango groves, through guava and litchi orchards, past broad-leaved sal and shisham trees. Once in the sal forest, Bansi turned the tonga on to a rough cart track, and we continued along it for about a furlong, until the road dipped down to the stream bed.

'Let us go straight into the water,' said Bansi. 'You and I and the pony!' And he drove the tonga straight into the middle of the stream, where the water came up to the pony's knees.

'I am not a great one for baths,' said Bansi, 'but the pony needs one, and why should a horse smell sweeter than its owner?' Saying that, he flung off his clothes and jumped into the water.

'Better than bathing under a tap!' he cried, slapping himself on the chest and thighs. 'Come down, dost, and join me!'

After some hesitation I joined him, but had some difficulty in keeping on my feet in the fast current. I grabbed at the pony's tail, and hung on to it, while Bansi began sloshing water over the patient animal's back.

After this, Bansi led both me and the pony out of the stream and together we gave the carriage a good washing down. I'd had a free ride and Bansi got the services of a free helper for the long overdue spring cleaning of his tonga. After we had finished the job, he presented me with a packet of aam pafiat—a sticky toffee made from mango pulp—and for some time I tore at it as a dog tears at a bit of old leather. Then I felt drowsy and lay down on the brown, sun-warmed grass. Crickets and grasshoppers were telephoning each other from tree and bush and a pair of bluejays rolled, dived and swooped acrobatically overhead.

Bansi had no watch. He looked at the sun and said, 'It is past three. When will that ayah of yours be home? She is more frightening than your grandmother!'

'She comes at four.'

'Then we must hurry back. And don't tell her where we've been, or I'll never be able to come to your house again. Your grandmother's one of my best customers.'

'That means you'd be sorry if she died.'

'I would indeed, my friend.'

Bansi raced the tonga back to town. There was very little motor traffic in those days, and tongas and bullock-carts were far more numerous than they are today.

We were back five minutes before Ayah returned. Before Bansi left, he promised to take me for another ride the following week.

◆

The house in Dehra had to be sold. My father had not left any money; he had never realized that his health would deteriorate so rapidly from the malarial fevers which had grown in frequency. He was still planning for the future when he died. Now that my father had gone, Grandmother saw no point in staying on in India; there was nothing left in the bank and she needed money for our passages to England, so the house had to go. Dr Ghose, who had a thriving medical practice in Dehra, made her a reasonable offer, which she accepted.

Then things happened very quickly. Grandmother sold most of our belongings, because as she said, we wouldn't be able to cope with a lot of luggage. The kabaris came in droves, buying our crockery, furniture, carpets and clocks at throwaway prices. Grandmother hated parting with some of her possessions, such as the carved giltwood mirror, her walnut-wood armchair and her rosewood writing desk, but it was impossible to take them with us. They were carried away in a bullock-cart.

Ayah was very unhappy at first but cheered up when

Grandmother got her a job with a tea-planter's family in Assam. It was arranged that she could stay with us until we left Dehra.

We left at the end of September, just as the monsoon clouds broke up, scattered and were driven away by soft breezes from the Himalayas. There was no time to revisit the island where my father and I had planted our trees. And in the urgency and excitement of the preparations for our departure, I forgot to recover my small treasures from the hole in the banyan tree. It was only when we were in Bansi's tonga, on the way to the station, that I remembered my top, catapult and Iron Cross. Too late! To go back for them would mean missing the train.

'Hurry!' urged Grandmother nervously. 'We mustn't be late for the train, Bansi.'

Bansi flicked the reins and shouted to his pony, and for once in her life Grandmother submitted to being carried along the road at a brisk trot.

'It's five to nine,' she said, 'and the train leaves at nine.'

'Do not worry, Memsahib. I have been taking you to the station for fifteen years, and you have never missed a train!'

'No,' said Grandmother. 'And I don't suppose you'll ever take me to the station again, Bansi.'

'Times are changing, Memsahib. Do you know that there is now a taxi—a *motor car*—competing with the tongas of Dehra? You are lucky to be leaving. If you stay, you will see me starve to death!'

'We will all starve to death if we don't catch that train,' said Grandmother.

'Do not worry about the train, it never leaves on time, and no one expects it to. If it left at nine o' clock, everyone would miss it.'

Bansi was right. We arrived at the station at five minutes

past nine, and rushed on to the platform, only to find that the train had not yet arrived.

The platform was crowded with people waiting to catch the same train or to meet people arriving on it. Ayah was there already, standing guard over a pile of miscellaneous luggage. We sat down on our boxes and became part of the platform life at an Indian railway station.

Moving among piles of bedding and luggage were sweating, cursing coolies; vendors of magazines, sweetmeats, tea and betel-leaf preparations; also stray dogs, stray people and sometimes a stray stationmaster. The cries of the vendors mixed with the general clamour of the station and the shunting of a steam engine in the yards. 'Tea, hot tea!' Sweets, papads, hot stuff, cold drinks, toothpowder, pictures of film stars, bananas, balloons, wooden toys, clay images of the gods—the platform had become a bazaar.

Ayah was giving me all sorts of warnings.

'Remember, baba, don't lean out of the window when the train is moving. There was that American boy who lost his head last year! And don't eat rubbish at every station between here and Bombay. And see that no strangers enter the compartment. Mr Wilkins was murdered *and* robbed last year!'

The station bell clanged, and in the distance there appeared a big, puffing steam engine, painted green and gold and black. A stray dog, with a lifetime's experience of trains, darted away across the railway lines. As the train came alongside the platform, doors opened, window shutters fell, faces appeared in the openings, and even before the train had come to a stop, people were trying to get in or out.

For a few moments there was chaos. The crowd surged backward and forward. No one could get out. No one could get in. A hundred people were leaving the train, two hundred were getting into it. No one wanted to give way.

The problem was solved by a man climbing out of a window. Others followed his example and the pressure at the doors eased and people started squeezing into their compartments.

Grandmother had taken the precaution of reserving berths in a first-class compartment, and assisted by Bansi and half a dozen coolies, we were soon inside with all our luggage. A whistle blasted and we were off! Bansi had to jump from the running train.

As the engine gathered speed, I ignored Ayah's advice and put my head out of the window to look back at the receding platform. Ayah and Bansi were standing on the platform, waving to me and I kept waving to them until the train rushed into the darkness and the bright lights of Dehra were swallowed up in the night. New lights, dim and flickering came into existence as we passed small villages. The stars too were visible and I saw a shooting star streaking through the heavens.

I remembered something that Ayah had once told me, that stars are the spirits of good men, and I wondered if that shooting star was a sign from my father that he was aware of our departure and would be with us on our journey. And I remembered something else that Ayah had said—that if one wished on a shooting star, one's wish would be granted, provided of course that one thrust all five fingers into the mouth at the same time!

'What on earth are you doing?' asked Grandmother staring at me as I thrust my hand into my mouth.

'Making a wish,' I said.

'Oh,' said Grandmother.

She was preoccupied, and didn't ask me what I was wishing for; nor did I tell her.

THE YOUNG REBEL

In 1950, my last year at school, I was the angry young man, in revolt against rules, traditions, conventions, examinations, authority of any kind. Obviously, the effects of the stilboestrol had worn off!

I was sixteen that year, and I felt I was wasting my time in school. Dickens hadn't done much schooling, I reasoned; nor had Jack London or Joseph Cornad or the Brontë sisters or other favourite authors. I had only to write a book and I would be in their glorious company! I'd been given charge of the Anderson Library, and it became my retreat and my private academy. I worked my way though the complete plays of George Bernard Shaw and J.M. Barrie, and devoured the novels of H.G. Wells, J.B. Priestley and the short stories of H.E. Bates, William Saroyan (who had recently burst on the scene) and A.E. Coppard. These last three probably influenced me more than any of the others, because over the years I was to find that the short story or novella best suited my temperament: snatching at life and recording its impressions and sensations rather than trying to digest it whole.

Most of that school year I was in perpetual revolt against authority. This was represented in the person of Mr Fisher, our new headmaster. He was a clever man, with a sharp mind, but he had no children of his own and seemed unable to understand children and their problems. You could confide in Mr Jones and even in one or two of the other teachers, but Fisher seemed to discourage any sort of relationship that would penetrate the invisible barrier he had thrown around himself. His wife was a plum pudding of a woman, who indulged in gross favouritism. The trouble was, this month's favourite would become next month's hate object and she would go out of her way to make trouble for those who had fallen from grace.

She'd called me a 'doodwalla' (milkman) for letting in a goal during a football match, and I'd retaliated by calling her a 'doodwalli' (milkmaid). For this I was caned, which was fair enough. After all, she was the headmaster's wife.

The food was indifferent that year and some of the boys in my house kept complaining. After all, I was their house captain! And so, the next time Fisher made his rounds of the dining hall, I complained in turn, saying the food was bad and that there wasn't enough of it. It wasn't exactly Oliver Twist asking for more: we were not starved. It was simply William Brown asking for better.*

For this, I lost my house captaincy for a time. But I suppose I had a certain amount of charm because I remember my English teacher, Mr Whitmarsh Knight, saying: 'I have a number of reasons for disliking you, Bond, but when I see you I can never remember what they are!'

And then, during the half-yearly exams, I'd submitted a blank answer paper in physics. I was quite hopeless in maths and science but Fisher, who taught the latter, took it as a personal affront. Not only did he give me a zero, he gave me two zeros. I still don't know what two zeros add up to but there must

---

*Read the *Just William* stories by Richmal Crompton.

be a rational scientific explanation for them. 0^2 must be more powerful than just 0, I'm sure. Dislike to the power of two equals hate!

Poor Fisher... A year later, when I was on my way to England, I heard that both he and his wife had been asked to leave the school—they'd been involved in some scandal or the other. She was the bigger hypocrite of the two, but perhaps the public school system was the biggest hypocrite of all. It set impossible standards for the boys—standards that the staff and administrators could not uphold. For they were frail and faulty humans like the rest of us.

During the next decade my old school went downhill. But I believe it has now recovered some of its old esteem.

◆

In December of 1950, I said goodbye to BCS forever, and swore that it was the end of my formal education. Henceforth, it would be conducted on my own in libraries and second-hand bookshops.

Looking back on the eight years of school in Simla, I find there is much to cherish in the memory—the friendships; the old library; the excursions to town. And yet, in India, it was so alien a setting (the 'Eton of the East'), and the life we led so far removed from the reality of the real India and its teeming cities and towns and endless rural horizons, that it did not give me the substance or the inspiration for any of my writing. Not a single story of any significance came out of my schooldays—this is the first time I have written about that period. There was nothing to hide. Worse, from the writer's point of view, there was nothing to reveal.

School behind me, I was all set to launch myself in the world as a writer. All glory comes from daring to begin!

Did I have any other ambitions? Oh, I would love to have been a tap-dancer like Gene Kelly or an Arsenal goalkeeper or a songwriter. But I was realist enough to know that in small-town India in 1951, you could go singin' in the rain but all you got for it was a cold.

There was the maidan, and of course I played a little football there and cricket too, for it was a nice big maidan in those days, without encroachments all over the place. Dehra's population was 40,000. Today it's ten times that! Ah, wilderness, where are you now?

There was one thing I could do in Dehra or anywhere else in the world, and that was write. All I needed was paper and pen or pencil. And that's all I need today. The pencil is my personal computer. All it requires is a good sharpener.

1951 was a watershed in my life; it was to see the genesis of my first novel, and it was to shape my character for the rest of my days.

Of personality I had none; not then, not ever! But I was very much my own person—strong in my likes and dislikes, very stubborn, wanting and getting my own way, my own room, my own privacy; old-fashioned enough to believe in loyalty to friends; scorning money for money's sake; ready to discover things about myself and come to terms with a wayward, sensual nature; above all, eager to express myself in the language I'd learnt to love; ambitious enough to want to see my name in print (if not in lights!). To love and be loved; to be free. Free to wander where I pleased; read what I liked; be friends with those who attracted me.

My ambition was tempered by a natural laziness.

Hands in my pockets, I loved to wander about the town: gaze at the film posters; browse at the bookstalls and news agencies; watch the wrestlers under the old peepal tree; savour the aromas of the bazaar; look at the trains arriving and departing at the station; admire the flowers from garden walls; watch the dhobis washing clothes on the canal banks; study a hoopoe looking for insects on a lawn; wander through the tea gardens; sit beside an irrigation channel and dream; whistle in the spring rain; eat hot pakoras; watch children playing marbles—anything but work!

And yet, I did write occasionally—a couple of atmospheric mystery stories in the manner of Peter Cheyney, which duly appeared (to be quickly forgotten) in a little magazine called *My Magazine of India*, published from Madras. I'd first try my stories out on *The Illustrated Weekly of India* or *The Sunday Statesman*. These were the most prestigious publications of the time. There weren't many others, unless you counted *The Onlooker* ('The Onlooker sees most of the game...'), a glossy society magazine modelled on the British *Tatler*, which kept you up to date about the more respectable activities of 'high society', chiefly in Bombay; you had to own a racehorse or two in order to be mentioned in its columns.

My rejects (of which there were quite a few) finally found their way into the pages of *My Magazine*, a strange little pocket magazine carrying advertisements for everything, from lucky gemstones to preparations for increasing male potency—all available by mail order. The actual stories were quite harmless, almost respectable, which made me suspect that it was the respectable people who were really interested in activating their sex drive.

My Magazine paid me the princely sum of rupees five per story. Quite rightly they called it an honorarium. I didn't mind. With five rupees I could see three pictures or buy two paperback novels or even a new gramophone record. I received a copy of the magazine every month—gratis, I thought. I'd even sent for a lucky gemstone, which turned out to be a piece of glass. But I took umbrage when I received a money order for two rupees, instead of the usual five, and wrote to the editor, objecting to this unwarranted reduction in my rate of payment. Back came a conciliatory note saying they hadn't reduced my fee, they had merely deducted a year's subscription from one of my payments. I was mollified.

Finally I sold a story to the *Weekly*—it was published later that year—and received a cheque for fifty rupees, which was as much as anyone paid for a story in those days.

♦

Before this momentous event, I had acquired a room of my own—a room on the roof of the old Gresham Hotel (now rented out as apartments)—and it came about in this way...

I had quarrelled with my mother. I forget what it was about, but I was touchy those days. I think I had been deprived of the use of the radiogram for a few days and had missed my favourite BBC comedy show—*Much-Binding-in-the-Marsh*—to which I had become somewhat addicted; that, and a growing resentment against my stepfather whose business ventures continued to flounder, along with his reputation; and I blurted out, 'Well, I'm not going to live here any longer,' and strode off into the sunset. And that too in late January, when Dehra was reeling under a cold wave, which meant I couldn't sleep in the open, on the maidan. I tried a bench on the platform of the railway station, where other vagrants lay bundled in blankets; but I hadn't brought a blanket, and sharing theirs wasn't a very inviting prospect. So I made my way to the flat of Dr Goyal, whose son, Bhim, a year or two younger than me, had just recently declared himself my friend, philosopher and guide.

He lived up to his declarations, sharing his dinner and small bedroom with me. We spent the night planning my future. I was to make some money by selling anything I had; then I was to find a job.

'But I don't have anything,' I said.

'What about all those books you got as prizes at school,' said Bhim. 'They're as good as new. We'll sell them at half price to Universal—he'll stick his own bookplate over yours, and sell the lot to the St Joseph's library.'

And this was what we did, with Bhim acting as a middleman. My new *Complete Shakespeare* (the Hailey Literature Prize), Hesketh Pearson's biography of Dickens (the Anderson Essay Prize) and several other books which had been picked up in the course of an erratic school career, found their way to the Universal Book Shop and eventually the St Joseph's library. The only book I hung on to was George and Weedon Grossmith's *Diary of a Nobody*, which I'd got for acting the part of a tipsy imposter in a one-act play called *Borrowed Plumes*. I had chosen this book myself, at Ram Advani's Bookshop on the Simla Mall. Tommy Handley, a BBC radio comedian, had mentioned that it was his favourite bedtime book, and that was recommendation enough for me. I loved its self-directed British humour, the sort that made Punch so popular in its heyday. I have always kept a copy with me.

Of course, Bhim took his commission on the money he got for the books. The rest, about a hundred rupees, lasted for a couple of days. In the company of Bhim and one or two others it melted away. I strolled home and announced to one and all (or to whoever was listening) that I would stay until I found a job; then settled down to a good helping of jackfruit curry and rice.

My mother and stepfather took the whole business very calmly, but it must have worried them, because it was soon after this that I was given my own room—a tiny *barsati*, opening on to the flat roof of the old building. A flight of stone steps ran up to it on the outside of the building. So it had its own entrance and was quite private—except for various birds, squirrels, bats and other small creatures which were also in residence in various corners of that spacious old roof.

A bed, a table and a chair were all that the room contained. It was all I needed—all that any writer needs. Even today, forty-five years later, my room contains the same basic furnishings—only the table is larger, to accommodate more in the way of paper and manuscripts; the bed is slightly more comfortable; and there is a rug on the floor. There is a separate room for my books—a major luxury.

Then, as now, the view from my room, or from its windows, has always been an important factor in my life and in my writing. I don't think I could stay anywhere for long unless there was a window from which to gaze out upon the world.

Of course, I had the entire roof to myself, but the window was important too. It set the scene, so to speak. From my little desk I could look into a bottle-brush tree, and then down the road into the litchi orchard behind old Mrs Wilson's house—over the trees and rooftops, as far as the foothills.

Mrs Wilson's late husband, Charlie, had earned a certain distinction by going to jail for fraud. It was said that he came out of jail a rich man, having bankrupted all his friends and associates. Charlie Wilson's father had been the famous 'Pahari' Wilson, who had made a fortune as the Raja of Tehri's contractor, being the first man to float timber down the Bhagirathi river. This made him the first large-scale exploiter of the forest wealth of this region. He married a village girl and built himself a splendid house at Harsil, eight thousand feet up the river valley. Capitalist villain or pioneering entrepreneur? It depends on how you look at these things. Legend has grown around Wilson but he was no romantic.

The area where the station canteen and other buildings stood had once been a large mango grove owned by the Wilsons, but Charlie had sold or lost most of it, and Mrs Wilson's bungalow was all that remained of a once beautiful estate.

Close by and of more interest to me, was a small bungalow where one of my friends, Ranbir, lived with his sister and mother. His father, a businessman, was away for long periods (another Charlie?) and the rent was often falling due (as, indeed, was ours), but they managed to sustain themselves on his occasional remittances. Ranbir's sister Raj was an attractive, athletic-looking Punjabi girl who enslaved me with one sidelong look from her dark, friendly but fiery eyes. My walks now underwent a sudden change of direction, so that I passed their house at least twice a day. Raj was often in her garden or courtyard, hanging out washing or watering flower beds, and I would stop to exchange a few pleasantries and bathe in the warmth of her frank, appraising gaze. She wouldn't have been called beautiful by those who expect a woman to be completely feminine; she probably had a few male chromosomes in her make-up, giving her the athletic figure that made her so attractive for me. Her face lit up in a smile whenever she saw me, and as no one objected to my visits, they became more frequent and I lingered longer at the hedge that separated her garden from the road. (Yes, we had hedges then, not walls—how times have changed!)

A sewing needle having penetrated her heel and moved some way into her foot, a minor operation was required to remove it. As a result, she had to rest on her bed for a few days. When I enquired about her welfare, I was invited in to see her.

I found Raj reclining, goddess-like, on a *charpai*, one bandaged foot on a pillow, the other elegant bare foot tracing patterns on the wall. She was in cheerful spirits and persuaded me to sit beside her and talk...which I did for as long as I could, there being nothing else I could do, with her mother in the next room and Ranbir kicking a football around in the courtyard. I longed to stroke her foot (either foot!) and even gave a hint to this effect, lying that I had taken a course in massage.

Raj said it might be possible later on, maybe when the foot was healed and out of its bandage! The other foot probably needed it too, I observed—there's nothing like a little massage to improve the circulation—but she said she had a headache and would rather sleep, so I went away, expressing the hope that the bandage would soon be removed.

The foot took some time to heal, and my visits grew longer and more solicitous. If patience is necessary to courting a girl, I had all the patience in the world. And Raj was always happy to see me. She allowed me to hold her hand when no one was about, and on one occasion, when her mother was busy in the kitchen, she asked me to put some Oriental balm on her forehead, as she was having one of her headaches. Wonderful stuff, Oriental balm, I have been loyal to it ever since! Using a generous amount of balm, I proceeded to rub it gently into that lovely forehead. Some of it got into her eyes and she cried out and pulled my hands away. I took the opportunity to kiss her eyelids and the palm of her hand.

And that was as far as I got, because Ranbir returned with his cricket bat and ball, demanding that I play with him. Wretched game, cricket, keeping romantic youths out in the sun when they should be indoors, applying balm to the foreheads of feverish young maidens.

But Raj was fond of games too, and when she was better, told me that we should start playing badminton. Did I play badminton? No, I said truthfully, but I was eager to learn, especially if she was to be my tutor.

I helped her to mark out a badminton court on a bit of wasteland behind the station canteen, and also found some old rackets and a net in Mr Hari's workshop. He had been a badminton player before taking up shikar!

It turned out that Raj had been a badminton champion at school, and as I was a novice at the game, I spent most of the time picking up the shuttlecock and returning it to her. The things we do for love! The scoreline usually went 15-0, 15-0, in her favour. As my game improved slightly, I edged up on her, but she was still beating me 15-2, 15-2! I did not mind. It was lovely to hear her laugh as the shuttlecock whizzed past my ear or caught me in the midriff.

She played barefoot on the dew-drenched early morning grass, and I shall always remember her that way as she darted about the badminton court, lissom, gazelle-like, sparkling in the sunrise. Sometimes I stood still in order to admire her and she would call out, 'What are you staring at? Why don't you play?'

If this were fiction, I would launch into a romantic story. But in small-town Dehra in 1951, you couldn't go anywhere with a girl, unless you wanted to ruin her reputation. You could play badminton with her outside her house, but you couldn't take her to the pictures or to a restaurant without being pursued by callow college students shouting obscenities.

One evening she came up to my room with her brother, and we sat out on the roof, under the stars, and talked of many things. When she left she took my hand in the dark and gave it a squeeze and bit me lightly on the cheek. Would that she had drawn blood!

We were friends—best of friends—but we could never be lovers.

MISS BABCOCK'S BIG TOE

If two people are thrown together for a long time, they can become either close friends or sworn enemies.

Thus it was with Tata and me when we both went down with mumps and had to spend a fortnight together in the school hospital. It wasn't really a hospital—just a five-bed ward in a small cottage on the approach road to our prep school in Chotta Simla. It was supervised by a retired nurse, an elderly matron called Miss Babcock who was all but stone deaf.

Miss Babcock was an able nurse, but she was a fidgety, fussy person, always dashing about from ward to dispensary, to her own room, and as a result the boys called her Miss Shuttlecock. As she couldn't hear us, she didn't mind. But her hearing difficulty did create something of a problem—both for her and for her patients. If someone in the ward felt ill late at night, he had to shout or ring a bell—and she heard neither. So someone had to get up and fetch her.

Miss Babcock devised an ingenious method of waking herself in an emergency. She tied a long piece of string to the foot of a sick person's bed; then took the other end of the string to her own room where, upon retiring for the night, she tied it to her big toe.

A vigorous pull on the string from the sick person, and Miss Babcock would be wide awake!

Now, what could be more tempting than this device? The string was tied to the foot of Tata's bed, and he was a restless fellow, always wanting water, always complaining of aches and pains. And sometimes, out of plain mischief, he would give several tugs on that string until Miss Babcock arrived with a pill or a glass of water.

'You'll have my toe off by morning,' she complained. 'You don't have to pull quite so hard.'

And what was worse, when Tata did fall asleep, he snored to high heaven and nothing could wake him! I had to lie awake most of the night, listening to his rhythmic snoring. It was like a trumpet tuning up. Or a bull-frog calling to its mate.

Fortunately, a couple of nights later, we were joined in the ward by Bimal, a friend and fellow 'feather', who had also contracted mumps. One night of Tata's snoring, and Bimal resolved to do something about it.

'Wait until he's fast asleep,' said Bimal, 'and then we'll carry his bed outside and leave him on the verandah.' We did more than that. As Tata commenced his nightly imitation of the all-wind instruments in the London Philharmonic Orchestra, we pushed up his bed as gently as possible and carried it out into the garden, putting it down beneath the nearest pine tree.

'It's healthier outside,' said Bimal, justifying our action. 'All this fresh air should cure him.'

Leaving Tata to serenade the stars, we returned to the ward and enjoyed a good night's sleep. So did Miss Babcock.

In fact, no one slept because we were woken by Miss Babcock running around the ward screaming 'Where's Tata, there was no sign.' Instead, a large black-faced langur sat at the foot of the bed, showing us its teeth in a grin of disfavour.

'Tata's gone,' gasped Miss Babcock.

'He must be a sleep-walker too,' said Bimal.

'Maybe the leopard took him,' I said. Just then there was a commotion in the shrubbery at the end of the garden, and shouting 'Help, help!' Tata emerged from the bushes, followed by several lithe, long-tailed langurs, merrily, giving chase. Apparently he'd woken up at the crack of dawn, to find his bed surrounded by a gang of inquisitive simians. They had meant no harm; but Tata had panicked, and made a dash for life and liberty, running into the forest instead of into the cottage. We got Tata and his bed back into the ward, and Miss Babcock took his temperature and gave him a dose of salts. Oddly enough, in all the excitement no one asked how Tata and his bed had travelled in the night. And strange to say, he did not snore the following night, so maybe the pine-scented night air really helped. Needless to say, we soon recovered from the mumps, and Miss Babcock's big toe received a well-deserved rest.

BREAKFAST AT BAROG

It's well over seventy years that I actually breakfasted at Barog, that little railway station on the Kalka–Simla line, but last night I dreamt of it—dreamt of the station, the dining room, the hillside and the long dark Barog tunnel—which meant that it had been present in my subconscious all these years and was now striving to come to the fore and revive a few poignant memories.

Should I go there again? The station is still there, and so is the tunnel. I'm told that the area has been built up over the years, so that it is now almost a mini hill station. That wouldn't surprise me. Our villages have become towns, our towns have become cities and in a few years' time our country will be one vast megacity with a few parks here and there to remind us that this was once a green planet.

I don't remember any dwellings around Barog, just that one little station and its one little restaurant with a cook and a waiter and its one little stationmaster. No, such a small station couldn't have had someone as important as a stationmaster. Someone quite junior must have been in charge.

Never mind. It was the breakfast that was important. And that I was with my father and on my way to Simla and a boarding school. The boarding school was the least desirable part of the journey. It was almost two years since I had been in a school and I was perfectly happy to continue living in an ideal world where schools need not exist. The breakup of my parents' marriage had resulted in my being withdrawn from a convent school in Mussoorie and taken over by my father who was on active service with the RAF. It was 1942 and World War II was at its peak. Against all regulations he kept me with him, but to do this he had to rent a flat in New Delhi. Most of the day he was at work and I would have the flat to myself, surrounded by books, gramophone records and stamp albums. Evenings I would help him with his stamp collection, for he was an avid collector. On weekends he would take me to see Delhi's historic monuments; there was no dearth of them. From the stamps I learnt geography, from the monuments history, from the books literature. I learnt more in two years at home than I did in a year at school.

But finally he was transferred—first Colombo, then Karachi, then Calcutta—and it was no longer possible for me to share his quarters. I was admitted to Bishop Cotton's in Simla.

We took the railcar from Kalka. It glided over the rails without any of the huffing and puffing of the steam engine that dragged the little narrow gauge train up the steep mountain. I would be travelling in that train in the years to come, but on this, my first to Simla, I was given the luxury of the railcar.

It glided into the Barog station punctually at 10 a.m., in time for breakfast.

The Barog breakfast was already well known and I did full justice to it. I skipped the cornflakes and concentrated on the scrambled eggs and buttered toasts. There was bacon too, and honey and marmalade.

'Tuck in, Ruskin,' said my father, 'School breakfasts won't be half as good.'

He didn't eat much himself. There was a lot on his mind in those days, apart from his work. There was his estranged wife, my mother; my invalid sister, now with his mother in Calcutta; his frequent transfers; his own frequent attacks of malaria; and our future in India, once the War was over—for India's Independence was just around the corner.

'When do we get to Simla?' I asked, quite happy to remain in Barog forever.

'In a little over an hour. But first we go through the longest of all the tunnels on this line. It will take about five minutes. Time for you to make a wish.'

The railcar plunged into the tunnel and we were enveloped in the darkness of the mountain. I held my father's hand. A couple of soldiers sitting behind us broke into a song from an earlier war.

'Pack up your troubles in your old kitbag,
And smile, smile, smile!'

A glimmer of daylight appeared at the end of the tunnel and then we were out in the sunshine and the pine-scented air.

'Did you make your wish?' asked my father.

I nodded, 'I wished that my mother would come back.'

He was silent for a few moments. 'Do you miss her a lot?'

'I don't miss her,' I said firmly. 'I'm always happy with you. But you miss her all the time. I don't like to see you so sad.'

'I've often asked her to come back,' he said. 'But it's up to her. She wants a different kind of life.'

And that was true. She was still very young—in her late twenties—and she enjoyed parties and dances and a busy social life. My father was in his forties. He liked staying at home, listening to classical music. When he took a holiday, he went in search of rare butterflies. My mother was a butterfly too—pretty, merry, fluttering here and there—but most unwilling to be displayed in a butterfly museum.

I suppose for most of us, big or small, life is just a succession of making mistakes and we spend most of our time trying to rectify them. Marriage was a mistake for both my parents. And I was a product of that mistake!

In the time he had, my father did his best for me. And how proud I was of him when he accompanied me down to my new school! He was wearing his dark blue RAF uniform with its flying officer's stripes, and uniforms, especially officers' uniforms, made a great impression amongst schoolboys in those wartime days. I was received with respect and curiosity. Word went around that my father was a fighter pilot and that he'd shot down dozens of Japanese planes! He was another Biggles, that fictional aviator. Nothing could have been further from reality. My father did not fly at all. He worked for a unit called Codes and Cyphers, helping to create new codes or breaking down enemy codes. It was important work and secret work but there was no glamour about it.

Not that I was averse to the glamour of being Biggles Junior. In my previous school I'd been something of an outsider and the Irish nuns hadn't cared much for a quiet, sensitive boy. Here I was made to feel I belonged and in no time at all I made a number of friends. It was already halfway through the school year but I had no difficulty in catching up with my classmates.

This was 'prep' school—junior school—and certainly more fun than senior school, still a couple of years away, would ever be... Still, I was always looking forward to the winter break, when I would be with my father again, for at least three months. And there he was, waiting at the Old Delhi railway station, as my train drew alongside the platform. He was still in Delhi, at Air Headquarters, and I made the most of my time with him. Connaught Place was close by, and two or three evenings every week, we would go to the cinema. There were four to choose from—the Regal, the Rivoli, the Odeon and the Plaza, all very new and smart and showing the latest films from Hollywood. I became a regular film buff. The bookshops were there too, and the record shops and Wenger's with its confectionery and the Milk Bar with its milkshakes and Kwality with its ice creams. It was hard to believe that there was a world war going on in Europe and Asia and North Africa and the Pacific; or that the Quit India movement was at its height and that my father and I might have to leave the country in the near future. He spoke about it sometimes and of the possibility of my going to a school in England. We did not talk about my mother, but I noticed that he still kept a photograph of her in his desk drawer.

It was back to school in March, when the rhododendrons were in bloom. This time I went up with the school party, in the small train with its steam engine chugging slowly up the steep inclines. The journey took all day. We did stop briefly at Barog, but we were not allowed to get down from the train; one or two boys were certain to be left behind. I looked longingly at the little restaurant on the far side of the platform; but it was already teatime. Breakfast was for the railcar!

The school year rolled on. My father was transferred to Karachi and then to Calcutta. He had grown up in Calcutta and knew the city well. He wrote to me every week and in his last letter he told me what I could look forward to during the winter holidays—the New Market with its bookshops, the botanical gardens with its ancient banyan tree, the zoo, the riverfront, the great maidan where hundreds of people would be taking in the evening air... I was hoping he would come up to see me during the autumn break, but instead I had news of another kind.

It must be difficult for a young schoolmaster, as yet

untouched by tragedy, to tell a ten-year-old that he has just lost his father. Mr Murtough was given this onerous duty. And he did his best, mumbling something ridiculous about God needing my father more than I did and so on and so on…

My friends were more natural in expressing this sympathy—giving me their sweets or chocolates, offering to play games with me, talking to me in the middle of the night when they discovered I wasn't asleep… For the future did look bleak. I wasn't sure where I would be going next—my Calcutta granny or my Dehra granny, or my mother and stepfather… I did receive a letter from my mother, telling me that my father had died of the malaria that had plagued him for years; but it was an unemotional letter and it did little to bring me comfort.

But I did go to her when school closed for the winter and I was to spend the next few years in my stepfather's home. But that's another story.

I continued my school in Simla, and every year in March, the small train would take me and my schoolmates up the mountain, through numerous tunnels and winding gradients, forests of pine and deodar, and we always stopped at Barog, before the biggest tunnel of all. But I never made another wish when passing through that tunnel.

That was over seventy years ago.

Is the railcar still running on that line? And do they still serve breakfast at Barog?

They say you should see Venice before you die. Or better still, Varanasi. But I'll settle for that little station among the pines. And if my father is standing on the platform, waiting for me, ready to take me by the hand, I'll be a small boy again and that railcar will take us to a different destination altogether.

THE PLAYING FIELDS OF SHIMLA

It had been a lonely winter for a twelve-year-old boy.
   I hadn't really got over my father's untimely death two years previously; nor had I as yet reconciled myself to my mother's marriage to the Punjabi gentleman who dealt in second-hand cars. The three-month winter break was over, I was almost happy to return to my boarding school in Shimla—that elegant hill station once celebrated by Kipling and soon to lose its status as the summer capital of the Raj in India.

It wasn't as though I had many friends at school. I had always been a bit of a loner, shy and reserved, looking out only for my father's rare visits—on his brief leaves from RAF duties—and to my sharing his tent or air force hutment outside Delhi or Karachi. Those unsettled but happy days would not come again. I needed a friend but it was not easy to find one among a horde of rowdy, pea-shooting fourth formers, who carved their names on desks and stuck chewing gum on the class teacher's chair. Had I grown up with other children, I might have developed a taste for schoolboy anarchy; but, in sharing my father's loneliness after his separation from my mother, I had turned into a premature adult. The mixed nature of my reading—Dickens, Richmal Crompton, Tagore and *Champion* and *Film Fun* comics—probably reflected the confused state of my life. A book reader was rare even in those pre-electronic times. On rainy days most boys played cards or Monopoly, or listened to Artie Shaw on the wind-up gramophone in the common room.

After a month in the fourth form I began to notice a new boy, Omar, and only because he was a quiet, almost taciturn person who took no part in the form's feverish attempts to imitate the Marx Brothers at the circus. He showed no resentment at the prevailing anarchy, nor did he make a move to participate in it. Once he caught me looking at him, and he smiled ruefully, tolerantly. Did I sense another adult in the class? Someone who was a little older than his years?

Even before we began talking to each other, Omar and I developed an understanding of sorts, and we'd nod almost respectfully to each other when we met in the classroom corridors or the environs of the dining hall or dormitory. We were not in the same house. The house system practised its own form of apartheid, whereby a member of, say, Curzon House was not expected to fraternize with someone belonging to Rivaz or Lefroy! Those public schools certainly knew how to clamp you into compartments. However, these barriers vanished when Omar and I found ourselves selected for the School Colts' hockey team—Omar as a fullback, I as goalkeeper. I think a defensive position suited me by nature. In all modesty I have to say that I made a good goalkeeper, both at hockey and football. And fifty years on, I am still keeping goal. Then I did it between goalposts, now I do it off the field—protecting a family, protecting my independence as a writer...

The taciturn Omar now spoke to me occasionally, and we combined well on the field of play. A good understanding is needed between goalkeeper and fullback. We were on the same wavelength. I anticipated his moves, he was familiar with mine.

Years later, when I read Conrad's *The Secret Sharer*, I thought of Omar.

It wasn't until we were away from the confines of school, classroom and dining hall that our friendship flourished. The hockey team travelled to Sanawar on the next mountain range, where we were to play a couple of matches against our old rivals, the Lawrence Royal Military School. This had been my father's old school, but I did not know that in his time it had also been a military orphanage. Grandfather, who had been a private foot soldier—of the likes of Kipling's Mulvaney, Otheris and Learoyd—had joined the Scottish Rifles after leaving home at the age of seventeen. He had died while his children were still very young, but my father's more rounded education had enabled him to become an officer.

Omar and I were thrown together a good deal during the visit to Sanawar and in our more leisurely moments, strolling undisturbed around a school where we were guests and not pupils, we exchanged life histories and other confidences. Omar, too, had lost his father—had I sensed that before?—shot in some tribal encounter on the Frontier, for he hailed from the lawless lands beyond Peshawar. A wealthy uncle was seeing to Omar's education. The RAF was now seeing to mine.

We wandered into the school chapel, and there I found my father's name—A.A. Bond—on the school's roll of honour board: old boys who had lost their lives while serving during the two world wars.

'What did his initials stand for?' asked Omar.

'Aubrey Alexander.'

'Unusual names, like yours. Why did your parents call you Ruskin?'

'I am not sure. I think my father liked the works of John

Ruskin, who wrote on serious subjects like art and architecture. I don't think anyone reads him now. They'll read me, though!' I had already started writing my first book. It was called *Nine Months* (the length of the school term, not a pregnancy), and it described some of the happenings at school and lampooned a few of our teachers. I had filled three slim exercise books with this premature literary project, and I allowed Omar to go through them. He must have been my first reader and critic. 'They're very interesting,' he said, 'but you'll get into trouble if someone finds them. Especially Mr Oliver.' And he read out an offending verse—

Oily, Oily, Oily, with his balls on a trolley,
And his arse all painted green!

I have to admit it wasn't great literature. I was better at hockey and football. I made some spectacular saves, and we won our matches against Sanawar. When we returned to Shimla, we were school heroes for a couple of days and lost some of our reticence; we were even a little more forthcoming with other boys. And then Mr Fisher, my housemaster, discovered my literary opus, *Nine Months,* under my mattress, and took it away and read it (as he told me later) from cover to cover. Corporal punishment then being in vogue, I was given six of the best with a springy malacca cane, and my manuscript was torn up and deposited in Fisher's waste-paper basket. All I had to show for my efforts were some purple welts on my bottom. These were proudly displayed to all who were interested, and I was a hero for another two days.

'Will you go away too when the British leave India?' Omar asked me one day.

'I don't think so,' I said. 'My stepfather is Indian.'

'Everyone is saying that our leaders and the British are going to divide the country. Shimla will be in India, Peshawar in Pakistan!'

'Oh, it won't happen,' I said glibly. 'How can they cut up such a big country?' But even as we chatted about the possibility, Nehru and Jinnah and Mountbatten and all those who mattered were preparing their instruments for major surgery.

Before their decision impinged on our lives and everyone else's, we found a little freedom of our own—in an underground tunnel that we discovered below the third flat.

It was really part of an old, disused drainage system, and when Omar and I began exploring it, we had no idea just how far it extended. After crawling along on our bellies for some twenty feet, we found ourselves in complete darkness. Omar had brought along a small pencil torch, and with its help we continued writhing forward (moving backwards would have been quite impossible) until we saw a glimmer of light at the end of the tunnel. Dusty, musty, very scruffy, we emerged at last on to a grassy knoll, a little way outside the school boundary.

It's always a great thrill to escape beyond the boundaries that adults have devised. Here we were in an unknown territory. To travel without passports—that would be the ultimate freedom!

But more passports were on their way and more boundaries.

Lord Mountbatten, Viceroy and Governor-General-to-be, came for our Founder's Day and gave away the prizes. I had won a prize for something or the other, and mounted the rostrum to receive my book from this towering, handsome man in his pinstripe suit. Bishop Cotton's was then the premier school of India, often referred to as the 'Eton of the East'. Viceroys and Governors had graced its functions. Many of its boys had gone on to eminence in the civil services and armed forces. There was one 'old boy' about whom they maintained a stolid silence—General Dyer, who had ordered the massacre at Amritsar and destroyed the trust that had been building up between Britain and India.

Now Mountbatten spoke of the momentous events that were happening all around us—the War had just come to an end, the United Nations held out the promise of a world living in peace and harmony, and India, an equal partner with Britain, would be among the great nations...

A few weeks later, Bengal and Punjab provinces were bisected. Riots flared up across northern India, and there was a great exodus of people crossing the newly drawn frontiers of Pakistan and India. Homes were destroyed, thousands lost their lives.

The common-room radio and the occasional newspaper kept us abreast of events, but in our tunnel, Omar and I felt immune from all that was happening, worlds away from all the pillage, murder and revenge. And outside the tunnel, on the pine knoll below the school, there was fresh untrodden grass, sprinkled with clover and daisies, the only sounds the hammering of a woodpecker, the distant insistent call of the Himalayan barbet. Who could touch us there?

'And when all the wars are done,' I said, 'a butterfly will still be beautiful.'

'Did you read that somewhere?'

'No, it just came into my head.'

'Already you're a writer.'

'No, I want to play hockey for India or football for Arsenal. Only winning teams!'

'You can't win forever. Better to be a writer.'

When the monsoon rains arrived, the tunnel was flooded, the drain choked with rubble. We were allowed out to the cinema to see Lawrence Olivier's *Hamlet*, a film that did nothing to raise our spirits on a wet and gloomy afternoon—but it was our last picture that year, because communal riots suddenly broke out in Shimla's Lower Bazaar, an area that was still much as Kipling had described it—'a man who knows his way there can defy all the police of India's summer capital'—and we were confined to school indefinitely.

One morning after chapel, the headmaster announced that the Muslim boys—those who had their homes in what was now Pakistan—would have to be evacuated, sent to their homes across the border with an armed convoy.

The tunnel no longer provided an escape for us. The bazaar was out of bounds. The flooded playing field was deserted. Omar and I sat on a damp wooden bench and talked about the future in vaguely hopeful terms; but we didn't solve any problems. Mountbatten and Nehru and Jinnah were doing all the solving.

It was soon time for Omar to leave—he along with some fifty other boys from Lahore, Pindi and Peshawar. The rest of us—Hindus, Christians, Parsis—helped them load their luggage into the waiting trucks. A couple of boys broke down and wept. So did our departing school captain, a Pathan who had been known for his stoic and unemotional demeanour. Omar waved cheerfully to me and I waved back. We had vowed to meet again some day,

The convoy got through safely enough. There was only one casualty—the school cook, who had strayed into an off-limits area in the foothill town of Kalka and been set upon by a mob. He wasn't seen again.

Towards the end of the school year, just as we were all getting ready to leave for the school holidays, I received a letter from Omar. He told me something about his new school and how he missed my company and our games and our tunnel to freedom. I replied and gave him my home address, but I did not hear from him again. The land, though divided, was still a big one, and we were very small.

Some seventeen or eighteen years later I did get news of Omar, but in an entirely different context. India and Pakistan were at war and in a bombing raid over Ambala, not far from Shimla, a Pakistani plane was shot down. Its crew died in the crash. One of them, I learnt later, was Omar.

Did he, I wonder, get a glimpse of the playing fields we knew so well as boys?

Perhaps memories of his schooldays flooded back as he flew over the foothills. Perhaps he remembered the tunnel through which we were able to make our little escape to freedom.

But there are no tunnels in the sky.

MY FATHER'S TREES IN DEHRA

Our trees still grow in Dehra. This is one part of the world where trees are a match for man. An old peepul may be cut down to make way for a new building; two peepul trees will sprout from the walls of the building. In Dehra the air is moist, the soil hospitable to seeds and probing roots. The valley of Dehra Dun lies between the first range of the Himalayas and the smaller but older Siwalik range. Dehra is an old town, but it was not in the reign of Rajput princes or Mogul kings that it really grew and flourished; it acquired a certain size and importance with the coming of British and Anglo-Indian settlers. The English have an affinity with trees, and in the rolling hills of Dehra they discovered a retreat which, in spite of snakes and mosquitoes, reminded them, just a little bit, of England's green and pleasant land.

The mountains to the north are austere and inhospitable; the plains to the south are flat, dry and dusty. But Dehra is green. I look out of the train window at daybreak to see the sal and shisham trees sweep by majestically, while trailing vines and great clumps of bamboo give the forest a darkness and density which add to its mystery. There are still a few tigers in these forests; only a few, and perhaps they will survive, to stalk the spotted deer and drink at forest pools.

I grew up in Dehra. My grandfather built a bungalow on

the outskirts of the town at the turn of the century. The house was sold a few years after Independence. No one knows me now in Dehra, for it is over twenty years since I left the place, and my boyhood friends are scattered and lost. And although the India of Kim is no more, and the Grand Trunk Road is now a procession of trucks instead of a slow-moving caravan of horses and camels, India is still a country in which people are easily lost and quickly forgotten.

From the station I can take either a taxi or a snappy little scooter rickshaw (Dehra had neither before 1950), but, because I am on an unashamedly sentimental pilgrimage, I take a tonga, drawn by a lean, listless pony, and driven by a tubercular old Muslim in a shabby green waistcoat. Only two or three tongas stand outside the station. There were always twenty or thirty here in the 1940s when I came home from boarding school to be met at the station by my grandfather. But the days of the tonga are nearly over, and in many ways this is a good thing, because most tonga ponies are overworked and underfed. Its wheels squeaking from lack of oil and its seat slipping out from under me, the tonga drags me through the bazaars of Dehra. A couple of miles of this slow, funereal pace makes me impatient to use my own legs, and I dismiss the tonga when we get to the small Dilaram Bazaar.

It is a good place from which to start walking.

The Dilaram Bazaar has not changed very much. The shops are run by a new generation of bakers, barbers and banias, but professions have not changed. The cobblers belong to the lower castes, the bakers are Muslims, the tailors are Sikhs. Boys still fly kites from the flat rooftops, and women wash clothes on the canal steps. The canal comes down from Rajpur and goes underground here, to emerge about a mile away.

I have to walk only a furlong to reach my grandfather's house. The road is lined with eucalyptus, jacaranda and laburnum trees. In the compounds there are small groves of mangoes, litchis and papayas. The poinsettia thrusts its scarlet leaves over garden walls. Every verandah has its bougainvillea creeper, every garden its bed of marigolds. Potted palms, those symbols of Victorian snobbery, are popular with Indian housewives. There are a few houses, but most of the bungalows were built by 'old India hands' on their retirement from the army, the police or the railways. Most of the present owners are Indian businessmen or government officials.

I am standing outside my grandfather's house. The wall has been raised, and the wicket gate has disappeared; I cannot get a clear view of the house and garden. The nameplate identifies the owner as Major General Saigal; the house has had more than one owner since my grandparents sold it in 1949.

On the other side of the road there is an orchard of litchi trees. This is not the season for fruit, and there is no one looking after the garden. By taking a little path that goes through the orchard, I reach higher ground and gain a better view of our old house.

Grandfather built the house with granite rocks taken from the foothills. It shows no sign of age. The lawn has disappeared; but the big jackfruit tree, giving shade to the side verandah, is still there. In this tree I spent my afternoons, absorbed in my *Magnets*, *Champions* and *Hotspurs*, while sticky mango juice trickled down my chin. (One could not eat the jackfruit unless it was cooked into a vegetable curry.) There was a hole in the bole of the tree in which I kept my pocket knife, top, catapult and any badges or buttons that could be saved from my father's RAF tunics when he came home on leave. There was also an

Iron Cross, a relic of the First World War, given to me by my grandfather. I have managed to keep the Iron Cross; but what did I do with my top and catapult? Memory fails me. Possibly they are still in the hole in the jackfruit tree; I must have forgotten to collect them when we went away after my father's death. I am seized by a whimsical urge to walk in at the gate, climb into the branches of the jackfruit tree and recover my lost possessions. What would the present owner, the major general (retired), have to say if I politely asked permission to look for a catapult left behind more than twenty years ago?

An old man is coming down the path through the litchi trees. He is not a major general but a poor street vendor. He carries a small tin trunk on his head, and walks very slowly. When he sees me, he stops and asks me if I will buy something. I can think of nothing I need, but the old man looks so tired, so very old, that I am afraid he will collapse if he moves any further along the path without resting. So I ask him to show me his wares. He cannot get the box off his head by himself, but together we manage to set it down in the shade, and the old man insists on spreading its entire contents on the grass; bangles, combs, shoelaces, safety pins, cheap stationery, buttons, pomades, elastic and scores of other household necessities.

When I refuse buttons because there is no one to sew them on for me, he plies me with safety pins. I say no; but as he moves from one article to another, his querulous, persuasive voice slowly wears down my resistance, and I end up buying envelopes, a letter pad (pink roses on bright blue paper), a one-rupee fountain pen guaranteed to leak and several yards of elastic. I have no idea what I will do with the elastic, but the old man convinces me that I cannot live without it.

Exhausted by the effort of selling me a lot of things I obviously do not want, he closes his eyes and leans back against the trunk of a litchi tree. For a moment I feel rather nervous. Is he going to die sitting here beside me? He sinks to his haunches and puts his chin on his hands. He only wants to talk.

'I am very tired, huzoor,' he says. 'Please do not mind if I sit here for a while.'

'Rest for as long as you like,' I say. 'That's a heavy load you've been carrying.'

He comes to life at the chance of a conversation and says, 'When I was a young man, it was nothing. I could carry my box up from Rajpur to Mussoorie by the bridle path—seven steep miles! But now I find it difficult to cover the distance from the station to Dilaram Bazaar.'

'Naturally. You are quite old.'

'I am seventy, sahib.'

'You look very fit for your age.' I say this to please him; he looks frail and brittle. 'Isn't there someone to help you?' I ask.

'I had a servant boy last month, but he stole my earnings and ran off to Delhi. I wish my son was alive—he would not have permitted me to work like a mule for a living—but he was killed in the riots in 1947.'

'Have you no other relatives?'

'I have outlived them all. That is the curse of a healthy life. Your friends, your loved ones, all go before you and in the end you are left alone. But I must go too, before long. The road to the bazaar seems to grow longer every day. The stones are harder. The sun is hotter in the summer, and the wind much colder in the winter. Even some of the trees that were there in my youth have grown old and have died. I have outlived the trees.'

He has outlived the trees. He is like an old tree himself, gnarled and twisted. I have the feeling that if he falls asleep in the orchard, he will strike root here, sending out crooked branches. I can imagine a small bent tree wearing a black waistcoat; a living scarecrow.

He closes his eyes again, but goes on talking.

'The English memsahibs would buy great quantities of elastic. Today it is ribbons and bangles for the girls, and combs for the boys. But I do not make much money. Not because I cannot walk very far. How many houses do I reach in a day? Ten, fifteen. But twenty years ago I could visit more than fifty houses. That makes a difference.'

'Have you always been here?'

'Most of my life, huzoor. I was here before they built the motor road to Mussoorie. I was here when the sahibs had their own carriages and ponies and the memsahibs their own rickshaws. I was here before there were any cinemas. I was here when the Prince of Wales came to Dehra Dun... Oh, I have been here a long time, huzoor. I was here when that house was built,' he says pointing with his chin towards my grandfather's house. 'Fifty, sixty years ago it must have been. I cannot remember exactly. What is ten years when you have lived seventy? But it was a tall, red-bearded sahib who built that house. He kept many creatures as pets. A kachwa (turtle) was one of them. And there was a python, which crawled into my box one day and gave me a terrible fright. The sahib used to keep it hanging from his shoulders, like a garland. His wife, the burra mem, always bought a lot from me—lots of elastic. And there were sons, one a teacher, another in the air force, and there were always children in the house. Beautiful children. But they went away many years ago. Everyone has gone away.'

I do not tell him that I am one of the 'beautiful children'. I doubt if he will believe me. His memories are of another age, another place, and for him there are no strong bridges into the present.

'But others have come,' I say.

'True, and that is as it should be. That is not my complaint. My complaint—should God be listening—is that I have been left behind.'

He gets slowly to his feet and stands over his shabby tin box, gazing down at it with a mix of disdain and affection. I help him to lift and balance it on the flattened cloth on his head. He does not have the energy to turn and make a salutation of any kind; but, setting his sights on the distant hills, he walks down the path with steps that are shaky and slow but still wonderfully straight.

I wonder how much longer he will live. Perhaps a year or two, perhaps a week, perhaps an hour. It will be an end of living, but it will not be death. He is too old for death; he can only sleep; he can only fall gently, like an old, crumpled brown leaf.

I leave the orchard. The bend in the road hides my grandfather's house. I reach the canal again. It emerges from under a small culvert, where ferns and maidenhair grow in the shade. The water, coming from a stream in the foothills, rushes along with a familiar sound; it does not lose its momentum until the canal has left the gently sloping streets of the town.

There are new buildings on this road, but the small police station is housed in the same old lime-washed bungalow. A couple of off-duty policemen, partly uniformed but with their pyjamas on, stroll about.

I cannot forget this little police station. Nothing very exciting ever happened in its vicinity until, in 1947, communal riots broke out in Dehra. Then, bodies were regularly fished out of the canal and dumped on a growing pile in the station compound. I was only a boy, but when I looked over the wall at that pile of corpses, there was no one who paid any attention to me. They were too busy to send me away. At the same time they knew that I was perfectly safe. While Hindus and Muslims were at each other's throats, a white boy could walk the streets in safety. No one was any longer interested in the Europeans.

The people of Dehra are not violent by nature, and the town has no history of communal discord. But when refugees from the partitioned Punjab poured into Dehra in thousands, the atmosphere became charged with tension. These refugees, many of them Sikhs, had lost their homes and livelihoods; many had seen their loved ones butchered. They were in a fierce and vengeful frame of mind. The calm, sleepy atmosphere of Dehra was shattered during two months of looting and murder. The Muslims who could get away, fled. The poorer members of the community remained in a refugee camp until the holocaust was over; then they returned to their former occupations, frightened and deeply mistrustful. The old boxman was one of them.

I cross the canal and take the road that will lead me to the riverbed. This was one of my father's favourite walks. He, too, was a walking man. Often, when he was home on leave, he would say, 'Ruskin, let's go for a walk,' and we would slip off together and walk down to the riverbed or into the sugarcane fields or across the railway lines and into the jungle.

On one of those walks (this was before Independence), I remember him saying, 'After the War is over, we'll be going to England. Would you like that?'

'I don't know,' I said. 'Can't we stay in India?'

'It won't be ours any more.'

'Has it always been ours?' I asked.

'For a long time,' he said, 'over two hundred years. But we have to give it back now.'

'Give it back to whom?' I asked. I was only nine.

'To the Indians,' said my father.

The only Indians I had known till then were my ayah and the cook and the gardener and their children, and I could not imagine them wanting to be rid of us. The only other Indian who came to the house was Dr Ghose, and it was frequently said of him that he was more English than the English. I could understand my father better when he said, 'After the War, there'll be a job for me in England. There'll be nothing for me here.'

The War had at first been a distant event; but somehow it kept coming closer. My aunt, who lived in London with her two children, was killed with them during an air raid; then my father's younger brother died of dysentery on the long walk out from Burma. Both these tragic events depressed my father. Never in good health (he had been prone to attacks of malaria), he looked more worn and wasted every time he came home. His personal life was far from being happy, as he and my mother had separated, she to marry again. I think he looked forward a great deal to the days he spent with me; far more than I could have realized at the time. I was someone to come back to; someone for whom things could be planned; someone who could learn from him.

Dehra suited him. He was always happy when he was among trees, and this happiness communicated itself to me. I felt like drawing close to him. I remember sitting beside him on the verandah steps when I noticed the tendril of a creeping vine that was trailing near my feet. As we sat there, doing nothing in particular—in the best gardens, time has no meaning—I found that the tendril was moving almost imperceptibly away from me and towards my father. Twenty minutes later it had crossed the verandah steps and was touching his feet. This, in India, is the sweetest of salutations.

There is probably a scientific explanation for the plant's behaviour—something to do with the light and warmth on the verandah steps—but I like to think that its movements were motivated simply by an affection for my father. Sometimes, when I sat alone beneath a tree, I felt a little lonely or lost. As soon as my father rejoined me, the atmosphere lightened, the tree itself became more friendly.

Most of the fruit trees round the house were planted by father; but he was not content with planting trees in the garden. On rainy days we would walk beyond the riverbed, armed with cuttings and saplings, and then we would amble through the jungle, planting flowering shrubs between the sal and shisham trees.

'But no one ever comes here,' I protested the first time. 'Who is going to see them?'

'Some day,' he said, 'someone may come this way... If people keep cutting trees, instead of planting them, there'll soon be no forests left at all, and the world will be just one vast desert.' The prospect of a world without trees became a sort of nightmare for me (and one reason why I shall never want to live on the treeless moon), and I assisted my father in his tree planting with great enthusiasm.

'One day the trees will move again,' he said. 'They've been standing still for thousands of years. There was a time when they could walk about like people, but someone cast a spell on them and rooted them to one place. But they're always trying to move—see how they reach out with their arms!'

We found an island, a small rocky island in the middle of a dry riverbed. It was one of those riverbeds, so common in the foothills, which are completely dry in the summer but flooded during the monsoon rains. The rains had just begun, and the stream could still be crossed on foot, when we set out with a number of tamarind, laburnum and coral tree saplings and cuttings. We spent the day planting them on the island, then ate our lunch there, in the shelter of a wild plum.

My father went away soon after that tree planting. Three months later, in Calcutta, he died.

I was sent to boarding school. My grandparents sold the house and left Dehra. After school, I went to England. The years passed, my grandparents died, and when I returned to India I was the only member of the family in the country.

And now I am in Dehra again, on the road to the riverbed. The houses with their trim gardens are soon behind me, and I am walking through fields of flowering mustard, which make a carpet of yellow blossom stretching away towards the jungle and the foothills.

The riverbed is dry at this time of the year. A herd of skinny cattle graze on the short brown grass at the edge of the jungle. The sal trees have been thinned out. Could our trees have survived? Will our island be there, or has some flash flood during a heavy monsoon washed it away completely?

As I look across the dry watercourse, my eye is caught by the spectacular red plumes of the coral blossom. In contrast with the dry, rocky riverbed, the little island is a green oasis. I walk across to the trees and notice that a number of parrots have come to live in them. A koel challenges me with a rising *who-are-you, who-are you.*

But the trees seem to know me. They whisper among

themselves and beckon me nearer. And looking around, I find that other trees and wild plants and grasses have sprung up under the protection of the trees we planted.

They have multiplied. They are moving. In this small forgotten corner of the world, my father's dreams are coming true, and the trees are moving again.

FRIENDS OF MY YOUTH

1
SUDHEER

Friendship is all about doing things together. It may be climbing a mountain, fishing in a mountain stream, cycling along a country road, camping in a forest clearing or simply travelling together and sharing the experiences that a new place can bring.

On at least two of these counts, Sudheer qualified as a friend, albeit a troublesome one, given to involving me in his adolescent escapades.

I met him in Dehra soon after my return from England. He turned up at my room, saying he'd heard I was a writer and did I have any comics to lend him?

'I don't write comics,' I said, but there were some comics lying around, left over from my own boyhood collection so I gave these to the lanky youth who stood smiling in the doorway, and he thanked me and said he'd bring them back. From my window I saw him cycling off in the general direction of Dalanwala.

He turned up again a few days later and dumped a large pile of new-looking comics on my desk. 'Here are all the latest,' he announced. 'You can keep them for me. I'm not allowed to read comics at home.'

It was only weeks later that I learnt he was given to pilfering comics and magazines from the town's bookstores. In no time at all, I'd become a receiver of stolen goods!

My landlady had warned me against Sudheer and so had one or two others. He had acquired a certain notoriety for having been expelled from his school. He had been in charge of the library, and before a consignment of newly acquired books could be registered and library stamped, he had sold them back to the bookshop from which they had originally been purchased. Very enterprising but not to be countenanced in a very pukka public school. He was now studying in a municipal school, too poor to afford a library.

Sudheer was an amoral scamp all right, but I found it difficult to avoid him, or to resist his undeniable and openly affectionate manner. He could make you laugh. And anyone who can do that is easily forgiven for a great many faults.

One day he produced a couple of white mice from his pockets and left them on my desk.

'You keep them for me,' he said. 'I'm not allowed to keep them at home.'

There were a great many things he was not allowed to keep at home. Anyway, the white mice were given a home in an old cupboard, where my landlady kept unwanted dishes, pots and pans, and they were quite happy there, being fed on bits of bread or chapati, until one day I heard shrieks from the storeroom, and charging into it, found my dear stout landlady having hysterics as one of the white mice sought refuge under her blouse and the other ran frantically up and down her back.

Sudheer had to find another home for the white mice. It was that, or finding another home for myself.

Most young men, boys and quite a few girls used bicycles.

There was a cycle hire shop across the road, and Sudheer persuaded me to hire cycles for both of us. We cycled out of town, through tea gardens and mustard fields, and down a forest road until we discovered a small, shallow river where we bathed and wrestled on the sand. Although I was three or four years older than Sudheer, he was much the stronger, being about six foot tall and broad in the shoulders. His parents had come from Bhanu, a rough and ready district on the North West Frontier, as a result of the partition of the country. His father ran a small press situated behind the Sabzi Mandi and brought out a weekly newspaper called *The Frontier Times*.

We came to the stream quite often. It was Sudheer's way of playing truant from school without being detected in the bazaar or at the cinema. He was sixteen when I met him, and eighteen when we parted, but I can't recall that he ever showed any interest in his school work.

He took me to his home in the Karanpur bazaar, then a stronghold of the Bhanu community. The Karanpur boys were an aggressive lot and resented Sudheer's friendship with an angrez. To avoid a confrontation, I would use the back alleys and side streets to get to and from the house in which they lived.

Sudheer had been overindulged by his mother, who protected him from his father's wrath. Both parents felt I might have an 'improving' influence on their son, and encouraged our friendship. His elder sister seemed more doubtful. She felt he was incorrigible, beyond redemption and that I was not much better, and she was probably right.

The father invited me to his small press and asked me if I'd like to work with him. I agreed to help with the newspaper for a couple of hours every morning. This involved proofreading and editing news agency reports. Uninspiring work, but useful.

Meanwhile, Sudheer had got hold of a pet monkey, and he carried it about in the basket attached to the handlebar of his bicycle. He used it to ingratiate himself with the girls. 'How sweet! How pretty!' they would exclaim, and Sudheer would get the monkey to show them its tricks.

After some time, however, the monkey appeared to be infected by Sudheer's amorous nature, and would make obscene gestures which were not appreciated by his former admirers. On one occasion, the monkey made off with a girl's dupatta. A chase ensued, and the dupatta retrieved, but the outcome of it all was that Sudheer was accosted by the girl's brothers and given a black eye and a bruised cheek. His father took the monkey away and returned it to the itinerant juggler who had sold it to the young man.

Sudheer soon developed an insatiable need for money. He wasn't getting anything at home, apart from what he pinched from his mother and sister, and his father urged me not to give the boy any money. After paying for my boarding and lodging I had very little to spare, but Sudheer seemed to sense when a money order or cheque arrived, and would hang around, spinning tall tales of great financial distress until, in order to be rid of him, I would give him five to ten rupees. (In those days, a magazine payment seldom exceeded fifty rupees.)

He was becoming something of a trial, constantly interrupting me in my work, and even picking up confectionery from my landlady's small shop and charging it to my account. I had stopped going for bicycle rides. He had wrecked one of the cycles and the shopkeeper held me responsible for repairs.

The sad thing was that Sudheer had no other friends. He did not go in for team games or for music or other creative pursuits which might have helped him to move around with people of his own age group. He was a loner with a propensity for mischief. Had he entered a bicycle race, he would have won easily. Forever eluding a variety of pursuers, he was extremely fast on his bike. But we did not have cycle races in Dehra.

And then, for a blessed two or three weeks, I saw nothing of my unpredictable friend.

I discovered later, that he had taken a fancy to a young schoolteacher, about five years his senior, who lived in a hostel up at Rajpur. His cycle rides took him in that direction. As usual, his charm proved irresistible, and it wasn't long before the teacher and the acolyte were taking rides together down lonely forest roads. This was all right by me, of course, but it wasn't the norm with the middle class matrons of small town India, at least not in 1957. Hostel wardens, other students and naturally Sudheer's parents, were all in a state of agitation. So I wasn't surprised when Sudheer turned up in my room to announce that he was on his way to Nahan, to study at an inter-college there.

Nahan was a small hill town about sixty miles from Dehra. Sudheer was banished to the home of his mama, an uncle who was a sub-inspector in the local police force. He had promised to see that Sudheer stayed out of trouble.

Whether he succeeded or not, I could not tell, for a couple of months later I gave up my rooms in Dehra and left for Delhi. I lost touch with Sudheer's family, and it was only several years later, when I bumped into an old acquaintance, that I was given news of my erstwhile friend.

He had apparently done quite well for himself. Taking off for Calcutta, he had used his charm and his fluent English to land a job as an assistant on a tea estate. Here he had proved quite efficient, earning the approval of his manager and employers.

But his roving eyes soon got him into trouble. The women working in the tea gardens became prey to his amorous and amoral nature. Keeping one mistress was acceptable. Keeping several was asking for trouble. He was found dead, early one morning, with his throat cut.

2
THE ROYAL CAFÉ SET

Dehra was going through a slump in those days, and there wasn't much work for anyone—least of all for my neighbour, Suresh Mathur, an income tax lawyer, who was broke for two reasons. To begin with, there was not much work going around, as those with taxable incomes were few and far between. Apart from that, when he did get work, he was slow and half-hearted about getting it done. This was because he seldom got up before eleven in the morning, and by the time he took a bus down from Rajpur and reached his own small office (next door to my rooms), or the Income Tax Office a little further on, it was lunchtime and all the tax officials were out. Suresh would then repair to the Royal Café for a beer or two (often at my expense) and this would stretch into a gin and tonic, after which he would stagger up to his first floor office and collapse on the sofa for an afternoon nap. He would wake up at six, after the Income Tax Office had closed.

I occupied two rooms next to his office, and we were on friendly terms, sharing an enthusiasm for the humorous works of P.G. Wodehouse. I think he modelled himself on Bertie Wooster for he would often turn up wearing mauve or yellow socks or a pink shirt and a bright green tie—enough to make anyone in his company feel quite liverish. Unlike Bertie Wooster, he did not have a Jeeves to look after him and get him out of various scrapes. I tried not to be too friendly, as Suresh was in the habit of borrowing lavishly from all his friends, conveniently forgetting to return the amounts. I wasn't well off and could ill afford the company of a spendthrift friend. Sudheer was trouble enough.

Dehra, in those days, was full of people living on borrowed money or no money at all. Hence, the large number of disconnected telephone and electric lines. I did not have electricity myself, simply because the previous tenant had taken off, leaving me with outstandings of over a thousand rupees, then a princely sum. My monthly income seldom exceeded five hundred rupees. No matter. There was plenty of kerosene available, and the oil lamp lent a romantic glow to my literary endeavours.

Looking back, I am amazed at the number of people who were quite broke. There was William Matheson, a Swiss journalist, whose remittances from Zurich never seemed to turn up; my landlady, whose husband had deserted her two years previously; Mr Madan, who dealt in second-hand cars which no one wanted; the owner of the corner restaurant, who sat in solitary splendour surrounded by empty tables; and the proprietor of the Ideal Book Depot, who was selling off his stock of unsold books and becoming a departmental store. We complain that few people buy or read books today, but I can assure you that there were even fewer customers in the fifties and sixties. Only doctors, dentists and the proprietors of English schools were making money.

Suresh spent whatever cash came his way, and borrowed more. He had an advantage over the rest of us—he owned an old bungalow, inherited from his father, up at Rajpur in the foothills, where he lived alone with an old manservant. And owning a property gave him some standing with his creditors. The grounds boasted of a mango and litchi orchard, and these he gave out on contract every year, so that his friends did not even get to enjoy some of his produce. The proceeds helped him to pay his office rent in town, with a little left over to give small amounts on account to the owner of the Royal Café.

If a lawyer could be hard up, what chance had a journalist? And yet, William Matheson had everything going for him from the start, when he came out to India as an assistant to Von Hesseltein, correspondent for some of the German papers. Von Hesseltein passed on some of the assignments to William, and for a time, all went well. William lived with Von Hesseltein and his family, and was also friendly with Suresh, often paying for the drinks at the Royal Café. Then William committed the folly (if not the sin) of having an affair with Von Hesseltein's wife. Von Hesseltein was not the understanding sort. He threw William out of the house and stopped giving him work.

William hired an old typewriter and set himself up as a correspondent in his own right, living and working from a room in the Doon Guest House. At first he was welcome there, having paid a three-month advance for room and board. He bombarded the Swiss and German papers with his articles, but there were very few takers. No one in Europe was really interested in India's five-year plans, or Corbusier's Chandigarh, or the Bhakra-Nangal Dam. Book publishing in India was confined to textbooks, otherwise William might have published a vivid account of his experiences in the French Foreign Legion. After two or three rums at the Royal Café, he would regale us with tales of his exploits in the Legion, before and after the siege of Dien Bien Phu. Some of his stories had the ring of truth, others (particularly his sexual exploits) were obviously tall tales;

but I was happy to pay for the beer or coffee in order to hear him spin them out.

Those were glorious days for an unknown freelance writer. I was realizing my dream of living by my pen, and I was doing it from a small town in North India, having turned my back on both London and New Delhi. I had no ambitions to be a great writer, or even a famous one, or even a rich one. All I wanted to do was *write*. And I wanted a few readers and the occasional cheque so I could carry on living my dream.

The cheques came along in their own desultory way—fifty rupees from the *Weekly*, or thirty-five from *The Statesman* or the same from *Sport and Pastime* and so on—just enough to get by, and to be the envy of Suresh Mathur, William Matheson and a few others; professional people who felt that I had no business earning more then they did. Suresh even declared that I should have been paying tax, and offered to represent me, his other clients having gone elsewhere.

And there was old Colonel Wilkie, living on a small pension in a corner room of the White House Hotel. His wife had left him some years before, presumably because of his drinking, but he claimed to have left her because of her obsession with moving the furniture—it seems she was always shifting things about, changing rooms, throwing out perfectly sound tables and chairs and replacing them with fancy stuff picked up here and there. If he took a liking to a particular easy chair and showed signs of settling down in it, it would disappear the next day to be replaced by something horribly ugly and uncomfortable.

'It was a form of mental torture,' said Colonel Wilkie, confiding in me over a glass of beer on the White House verandah. 'The sitting room was cluttered with all sorts of ornamental junk and flimsy side tables, so that I was constantly falling over the damn things. It was like a minefield! And the mines were never in the same place. You've noticed that I walk with a limp?'

'First World War?' I ventured. 'Wounded at Ypres? Or was it Flanders?'

'Nothing of the sort,' snorted the colonel. 'I did get one or two flesh wounds but they were nothing as compared to the damage inflicted on me by those damned shifting tables and chairs. Fell over a coffee table and dislocated my shoulder. Then broke an ankle negotiating a stool that was in the wrong place. Bookshelf fell on me. Tripped on a rolled up carpet. Hit by a curtain rod. Would you have put up with it?'

'No,' I had to admit.

'Had to leave her, of course. She went off to England. Send her an allowance. Half my pension! All spent on furniture!'

'It's a superstition of sorts, I suppose. Collecting things.'

The colonel told me that the final straw was when his favourite spring bed had suddenly been replaced by a bed made up of hard wooden slats. It was sheer torture trying to sleep on it, and he had left his house and moved into the White House Hotel as a permanent guest.

Now he couldn't allow anyone to touch or tidy up anything in his room. There were beer stains on the tablecloth, cobwebs on his family pictures, dust on his books, empty medicine bottles on his dressing table and mice nesting in his old, discarded boots. He had gone to the other extreme and wouldn't have anything changed or moved in his room.

I didn't see much of the room because we usually sat out on the verandah, waited upon by one of the hotel bearers, who came over with bottles of beer that I dutifully paid for, the colonel having exhausted his credit. I suppose he was in his late sixties then. He never went anywhere, not even for a walk in the compound. He blamed this inactivity on his gout, but it was really inertia and an unwillingness to leave the precincts of the bar, where he could cadge the occasional drink from a sympathetic guest. I am that age now, and not half as active as I used to be, but there are people to live for, and tales to tell, and I keep writing. It is important to keep writing.

Colonel Wilkie had given up on life. I suppose he could have gone off to England, but he would have been more miserable there, with no one to buy him a drink (since he wasn't likely to reciprocate), and the possibility of his wife turning up again to rearrange the furniture.

3
'BIBIJI'

My landlady was a remarkable woman, and this little memoir of Dehra in the 1950s would be incomplete without a sketch of hers.

She would often say, 'Ruskin, one day you must write my life story,' and I would promise to do so. And although she really deserves a book to herself, I shall try to do justice to her in these few pages.

She was, in fact, my Punjabi stepfather's first wife. Does that sound confusing? It was certainly complicated. And you might well ask, why on earth were you living with your stepfather's first wife instead of your stepfather and mother?

The answer is simple. I got on rather well with this rotund, well-built lady and sympathized with her predicament. She had been married at a young age to my stepfather, who was something of a playboy, and who ran the photographic saloon he had received as part of her dowry. When he left her for my mother, he sold the saloon and gave his first wife part of the premises. In order to sustain herself and two small children, she started a small provision store and thus became Dehra's first lady shopkeeper.

I had just started freelancing from Dehra and was not keen on joining my mother and stepfather in Delhi. When 'Bibiji'—as I called her—offered me a portion of her flat on very reasonable terms, I accepted without hesitation and was to spend the next two years above her little shop on Rajpur Road. Almost fifty years later, the flat in still there, but it is now an ice cream parlour! Poetic justice, perhaps.

'Bibiji' sold the usual provisions. Occasionally, I lent a helping hand and soon learnt the names of the various lentils arrayed before us—moong, malka, masoor, arhar, channa, rajma, etc. She bought her rice, flour and other items wholesale from the mandi, and sometimes I would accompany her on an early morning march to the mandi (about two miles distant) where we would load a handcart with her purchases. She was immensely strong and could lift sacks of wheat or rice that left me gasping. I can't say I blame my rather skinny stepfather for staying out of her reach.

She had a helper, a Bihari youth, who would trundle the cart back to the shop and help with the loading and unloading. Before opening the shop (at around 8 a.m.) she would make our breakfast—parathas with my favourite shalgam pickle, and in winter, a delicious kanji made from the juice of red carrots. When the shop opened, I would go upstairs to do my writing while she conducted the day's business.

Sometimes she would ask me to help her with her accounts, or in making out a bill, for she was barely literate. But she was an astute shopkeeper; she knew instinctively, who was good for credit and who was strictly nakad (cash). She would also warn me against friends who borrowed money without any intention of returning it; warnings that I failed to heed. Friends in perpetual need there were aplenty—Sudheer, William, Suresh and a couple of others—and I am amazed that I didn't have to borrow too, considering the uncertain nature of my income. Those little cheques and money orders from magazines did not always arrive in time. But sooner or later something *did* turn up. I was very lucky.

Bibiji had a friend, a neighbour, Mrs Singh, an attractive woman in her thirties who smoked a hookah and regaled us with tales of ghosts and chudails from her village near Agra. We did not see much of her husband who was an excise inspector. He was busy making money.

Bibiji and Mrs Singh were almost inseparable, which was quite understandable in view of the fact that both had absentee husbands. They were really happy together. During the day, Mrs Singh would sit in the shop, observing the customers. And afterwards she would entertain us to clever imitations of the more odd or eccentric among them. At night, after the shop was closed, Bibiji and her friend would make themselves comfortable on the same cot (creaking beneath their combined weights), wrap themselves in a razai or blanket and invite me to sit on the next charpoy and listen to their yarns or tell them a few of my own. Mrs Singh had a small son, not very bright, who was continually eating laddoos, jalebis, barfis and other sweets. Quite appropriately, he was called Laddoo. And, I believe, he grew into one.

Bibiji's son and daughter were then at a residential school. They came home occasionally. So did Mr Singh, with more sweets for his son. He did not appear to find anything unusual in his wife's intimate relationship with Bibiji. His mind was obviously on other things.

Bibiji and Mrs Singh both made plans to get me married. When I protested, saying I was only twenty-three, they said I was old enough. Bibiji had an eye on an Anglo-Indian schoolteacher who sometimes came to the shop, but Mrs Singh turned her down, saying she had very spindly legs. Instead, she suggested the daughter of the local padre, a glamourous-looking, dusky beauty, but Bibiji vetoed the proposal, saying the young lady used too much make-up and already displayed too much fat around the waistline. Both agreed that I should marry a plain-looking girl who could cook, use a sewing machine and speak a little English.

'And be strong in the legs,' I added, much to Mrs Singh's approval.

They did not know it, but I was enamoured of Kamla, a girl from the hills, who lived with her parents in quarters behind the flat. She was always giving me mischievous glances with her dark, beautiful, expressive eyes. And whenever I passed her on the landing, we exchanged pleasantries and friendly banter; it was as though we had known each other for a long time. But she was already betrothed, and that too to a much older man, a widower, who owned some land outside the town. Kamla's family was poor, her father was in debt and it was to be a marriage of convenience. There was nothing much I could do about it—landless, and without prospects—but after the marriage had taken place and she had left for her new home, I befriended her younger brother and through him sent her my good wishes from time to time. She is just a distant memory now, but a bright one, like a forget-me-not blooming on a bare rock. Would I have married her had I been able to? She was simple, unlettered, but I might have taken the chance.

Those two years on Rajpur Road were an eventful time, what with the visitations of Sudheer, the company of William and Suresh, the participation in Bibiji's little shop, the evanescent friendship with Kamla. I did a lot of writing and even sold a few stories here and there; but the returns were modest, barely adequate. Everyone was urging me to try my luck in Delhi. And so I bid goodbye to sleepy little Dehra (as it then was) and took a bus to the capital. I did no better there as a writer, but I found a job of sorts and that kept me going for a couple of years.

But to return to Bibiji, I cannot just leave her in limbo. She continued to run her shop for several years, and it was only failing health that forced her to close it. She sold the business and went to live with her married daughter in New Delhi. I saw her from time to time. In spite of high blood pressure, diabetes and eventually blindness, she lived on into her eighties. She was always glad to see me, and never gave up trying to find a suitable bride for me.

The last time I saw her, shortly before she died, she said, 'Ruskin, there is this widow—a lady who lives down the road and comes over sometimes. She has two children but they are grown up. She feels lonely in her big house. If you like, I'll talk to her. Its time you settled down. And she's only sixty.'

'Thanks, Bibiji,' I said, holding both ears. 'But I think I'll settle down in my next life.'

HOW FAR IS THE RIVER?

Between the boy and the river was a mountain. I was a small boy, and it was a small river, but the mountain was big.

The thickly forested mountain hid the river, but I knew it was there and what it looked like. I had never seen the river with my own eyes, but from the villagers I had heard of it, of the fish in its waters, of its rocks and currents and waterfalls, and it only remained for me to touch the water and know it personally.

I stood in front of our house on the hill opposite the mountain, and gazed across the valley, dreaming of the river. I was barefooted; not because I couldn't afford shoes, but because I felt free with my feet bare—because I liked the feel of warm stones and cool grass, because not wearing shoes saved me the trouble of taking them off.

It was eleven o'clock and I knew my parents wouldn't be home till evening. There was a loaf of bread I could take with me, and on the way I might find some fruit. Here was the chance I had been waiting for; it would not come again for a long time, because it was seldom that my father and mother visited friends for the entire day. If I came back before dark, they wouldn't know where I had been.

I went into the house and wrapped the loaf of bread in a newspaper. Then I closed all the doors and windows.

The path to the river dropped steeply into the valley, then rose and went round the big mountain. It was frequently used by the villagers, woodcutters, milkmen, shepherds, mule drivers—but there were no villages beyond the mountain or near the river.

I passed a woodcutter and asked him how far it was to the river. He was a short, powerful man, with a creased and weathered face, and muscles that stood out in hard lumps.

'Seven miles,' he said. 'Why do you want to know?'

'I am going there,' I said.

'Alone?'

'Of course.'

'It will take you three hours to reach it, and then you have to come back. It will be getting dark, and it is not an easy road.'

'But I'm a good walker,' I said, though I had never walked further than the two miles between our house and my school. I left the woodcutter on the path, and continued down the hill.

It was a dizzy, winding path, and I slipped once or twice and slid into a bush or down a slope of slippery pine needles. The hill was covered with lush green ferns, the trees were entangled in creepers and a great wild dahlia would suddenly rear its golden head from the leaves and ferns.

Soon I was in the valley, and the path straightened out and then began to rise. I met a girl who was coming from the opposite direction. She held a long curved knife with which she had been cutting grass, and there were rings in her nose and ears and her arms were covered with heavy bangles. The bangles made music when she moved her wrists. It was as though her hands spoke a language of their own.

'How far is it to the river?' I asked.

The girl had probably never been to the river, or she may

have been thinking of another one, because she said, 'Twenty miles,' without any hesitation.

I laughed and ran down the path. A parrot screeched suddenly, flew low over my head, a flash of blue and green. It took the course of the path, and I followed its dipping flight, running until the path rose and the bird disappeared amongst the trees.

A trickle of water came down the hillside, and I stopped to drink. The water was cold and sharp but very refreshing. But I was soon thirsty again. The sun was striking the side of the hill, and the dusty path became hotter, the stones scorching my feet. I was sure I had covered half the distance: I had been walking for over an hour.

Presently, I saw another boy ahead of me driving a few goats down the path.

'How far is the river?' I asked.

The village boy smiled and said, 'Oh, not far, just round the next hill and straight down.'

Feeling hungry, I unwrapped my loaf of bread and broke it in two, offering one half to the boy. We sat on the hillside and ate in silence.

When we had finished, we walked on together and began talking; and talking I did not notice the smarting of my feet and the heat of the sun, the distance I had covered and the distance I had yet to cover. But after some time my companion had to take another path, and once more I was on my own.

I missed the village boy; I looked up and down the mountain path but no one else was in sight. My own home was hidden from view by the side of the mountain, and there was no sign of the river. I began to feel discouraged. If someone had been with me, I would not have faltered; but alone, I was conscious of my fatigue and isolation.

But I had come more than half way, and I couldn't turn back; I had to see the river. If I failed, I would always be a little ashamed of the experience. So I walked on, along the hot, dusty, stony path, past stone huts and terraced fields, until there were no more fields or huts, only forest and sun and loneliness. There were no men, and no sign of man's influence—only trees and rocks and grass and small flowers and silence...

The silence was impressive and a little frightening. There was no movement, except for the bending of grass beneath my feet, and the circling of a hawk against the blind blue of the sky.

Then, as I rounded a sharp bend, I heard the sound of water. I gasped with surprise and happiness, and began to run. I slipped and stumbled, but I kept on running, until I was able to plunge into the snow-cold mountain water.

And the water was blue and white and wonderful.

FOUR BOYS ON A GLACIER

On a day that promised rain we bundled ourselves into the bus that was to take us to Kapkote (where people lost their caps and coats, punned Anil), the starting-point of our Himalayan trek. I was seventeen at the time, and Anil and Somi were sixteen. Each of us carried a haversack, and we had also brought along a good-sized bedding-roll which, apart from blankets, contained bags of rice and flour, thoughtfully provided by Anil's mother. We had no idea how we would carry the bedding-roll once we started walking, but we didn't worry too much about details.

We were soon in the hills of Kumaon, on a winding road that took us up and up, until we saw the valley and our small town spread out beneath us, the river a silver ribbon across the plain. We took a sharp bend, the valley disappeared, and the mountains towered above us.

At Kapkote we had refreshments and the shopkeeper told us we could spend the night in one of his rooms. The surroundings were pleasant, the hills wooded with deodars, the lower slopes planted with fresh green paddy. At night there was a wind moaning in the trees and it found its way through the cracks in the windows and eventually through our blankets.

Next morning we washed our faces at a small stream near the shop and filled our water bottles for the day's march. A boy from the nearby village approached us, and asked where we were going.

'To the glacier,' said Somi.

I'll come with you,' said the boy. 'I know the way.'

'You're too small,' said Anil. 'We need someone who can carry our bedding-roll.'

'I'm small but I'm strong,' said the boy, who certainly looked sturdy. He had pink cheeks and a well-knit body.

'See!' he said, and, picking up a rock the size of a football, he heaved it across the stream.

'I think he can come with us,' I said.

And then, we were walking—at first above the little Sarayu river, then climbing higher along the rough mule track, always within sound of the water, which we glimpsed now and then, swift, green and bubbling.

We were at the forest rest house by six in the evening, after covering fifteen miles. Anil found the watchman asleep in a patch of fading sunlight and roused him. The watchman, who hadn't been bothered by visitors for weeks, grumbled at our intrusion but opened a room for us. He also produced some potatoes from his store, and these were roasted for dinner.

Just as we were about to get into our beds we heard a thud on the corrugated tin roof, and then the sound of someone—or something—scrambling about on the roof. Anil, Somi and I were alarmed; but Bisnu, who was already under the blankets, merely yawned, and turned over on his side.

'It's only a bear,' he said. 'Didn't you see the pumpkins on the roof? Bears love pumpkins.'

For half an hour we had to listen to the bear as it clambered about on the roof, feasting on the watchman's ripe pumpkins. At last there was silence. Anil and I crawled out of our blankets and went to the window. And through the frosted glass we saw a black Himalayan bear ambling across the slope in front of the house.

Our next rest house lay in a narrow valley, on the banks of the rushing Pindar river, which twisted its way through the mountains. We walked on, past terraced fields and small stone houses, until there were no more fields or houses, only forest and sun and silence.

It was different from the silence of a room or an empty street.

And then, the silence broke into sound—the sound of the river.

Far down in the valley, the Pindar tumbled over itself in its impatience to reach the plains. We began to run, slipped and stumbled, but continued running.

The rest house stood on a ledge just above the river, and the sound of the water rushing down the mountain-defile could be heard at all times. The sound of the birds, which we had grown used to, was drowned by the sound of the water, but the birds themselves could be seen, many-coloured, standing out splendidly against the dark green forest foliage—the red crowned jay, the paradise flycatcher, the purple whistling thrush and others we could not recognize.

Higher up the mountain, above some terraced land where oats and barley were grown, stood a small cluster of huts. This, we were told by the watchman, was the last village on the way to the glacier. It was, in fact, one of the last villages in India, because if we crossed the difficult passes beyond the glacier, we would find ourselves in Tibet.

Anil asked the watchman about the Abominable Snowman. The Nepalese believe in the existence of the Snowman, and our watchman was Nepalese.

'Yes, I have seen the yeti,' he told us. 'A great shaggy,

flat-footed creature. In the winter, when it snows heavily, he passes the bungalow at night. I have seen his tracks the next morning.'

'Does he come this way in the summer?' asked Somi, anxiously.

'No,' said the watchman. 'But sometimes I have seen the *lidini*. You have to be careful of her.'

'And who is the *lidini?*' asked Anil.

'She is the snow-woman, and far more dangerous. She has the same height as the yeti—about seven feet when her back is straight—and her hair is much longer. Also she has very long teeth. Her feet face inwards, but she can run very fast, especially downhill. If you see a *lidini,* and she chases you, always run in an uphill direction. She tires quickly because of her crooked feet. But when running downhill she has no trouble at all, and you want to be very fast to escape her!'

'Well, we are quite fast,' said Anil with a nervous laugh. 'But it's just a fairy-story, I don't believe a word of it.'

The watchman was most offended, and refused to tell us anything more about snowmen and snow-women. But he helped Bisnu make a fire, and presented us with a black, sticky sweet, which we ate with relish.

It was a fine, sunny morning when we set out to cover the last seven miles to the glacier. We had expected a stiff climb, but the rest-house was 11,000 feet above sea-level, and the rest of the climb was fairly gradual.

Suddenly, abruptly, there were no more trees. As the bungalow dropped out of sight, the trees and bushes gave way to short grass and little pink and blue alpine flowers. The snow peaks were close now, ringing us in on every side. We passed white waterfalls, cascading hundreds of feet down precipitous rock faces, thundering into the little river. A great white eagle hovered over us.

The hill fell away, and there, confronting us, was a great white field of snow and ice, cradled between two shining peaks. We were speechless for several minutes. Then we proceeded cautiously on to the snow, supporting each other on the slippery surface. We could not go far, because we were quite unequipped for any high-altitude climbing. But it was a satisfying feeling to know that we were the only young men from our town who had walked so far and so high.

The sun was reflected sharply from the snow and we felt surprisingly warm. It was delicious to feel the sun crawling over our bodies, sinking deep into our bones. Meanwhile, almost imperceptibly, clouds had covered some of the peaks, and white mist drifted down the mountain slopes. It was time to return: we would barely make it to the bungalow before it grew dark.

We took our time returning to Kapkote—stopped by the Sarayu river; bathed with the village boys we had seen on the way up; collected strawberries and ferns and wild flowers; and finally said goodbye to Bisnu.

Anil wanted to take Bisnu along with us, but the boy's parents refused to let him go, saying that he was too young for the life of a city.

'Never mind,' said Somi. 'We'll go on another trek next year, and we'll take you with us, Bisnu.'

This promise pleased Bisnu, and he saw us off at the bus-stop, shouldering our bedding-roll to the end. Then he climbed a pine tree to have a better view of us leaving. We saw him waving to us from the tree as the bus went round the bend from Kapkote, and then the hills were left behind and the plains stretched out below.

THE DEHRA I KNOW

Formally, it's known as Dehra Dun, but in the 1940s and '50s, when we were young, everyone called it Dehra.

That's where I spent much of my childhood, boyhood and early manhood, and it was the Dehra I wrote about in many of my books and stories.

It was very different from the Dehra Dun of today—much smaller, much greener, considerably less crowded; sleepier too, and somewhat laid-back, easy-going; fond of gossip, but tolerant of human foibles. A place of bicycles and pony-drawn tongas. Only a few cars; no three-wheelers. And you could walk almost anywhere, at any time of the year, night or day.

The Dehra I knew really fell into three periods. The Dehra of my childhood, staying in my grandmother's house on the Old Survey Road (not much left of that bungalow now). The Dehra of my schooldays, when I would come home for the holidays to stay with my mother and stepfather—a different house on almost every visit, right up until the time I left for England. And then the Dehra of my return to India, when I lived on my own in a small flat above Astley Hall and wrote many of my best stories.

While I was in England, I wrote my first novel *The Room on the Roof*, which was all about the Dehra I had left and the people and young friends I had known and loved. It was a little immature, but it came straight from the heart—the heart and mind of a seventeen-year-old—and if it's still fresh today, fifty years after its first publication, it's probably because it was so spontaneous and unsophisticated.

Back in Dehra, I wrote a sequel of sorts, *Vagrants in the Valley*. It wasn't as good, probably because I had exhausted my adolescence as a subject for fiction; but it did capture aspects of life in Dehra and the Doon valley in the early '50s.

I had returned to India and Dehra when I was twenty-one, and set up my writing shop, so to speak, in that flat above Bibiji's provision store.

Bibiji was my stepfather's first wife. He and my mother had moved to Delhi, leaving Bibiji with the provision store. I got on very well with her and helped her with her accounts, and she gave me the use of her rooms above the shop. I think it's only in India that you could find such a situation—a young offspring of the Raj, somewhat at odds with his mother and Indian stepfather, choosing to live with the latter's abandoned first wife!

Bibiji made excellent parathas, shalgam (turnip) pickle and kanji, a spicy carrot juice. And so, romantic though I may have been, I was far from being the young poet starving in a garret, nor was Bibiji to be pitied. She was Dehra's first woman shopkeeper, and she managed very well.

Bibiji was of course much older than me; heavily built, strong. She could toss sacks of flour about the shop. Her son, rather mischievous, kept out of her reach; a cuff about the ears would send him sprawling. She suffered from a hernia, and was immensely grateful to me for bringing her a hernia-belt from England—it provided her with considerable relief.

Early morning she would march off to the mandi to get her

provisions (rice, atta, pulses, etc.) wholesale, and occasionally I would accompany her. In this way, I learnt the names of different pulses and lentils—moong, urad, malka, arhar, masoor, channa, lobia, rajma, etc. But I've never been tempted to write a cook book or run a ration-shop of my own.

I was quite happy cooking up stories, most of them written after dark by the light of a kerosene lantern. Bibiji hadn't been able to pay the flat's accumulated electricity bills, and as a result the connection had been cut. But this did not bother me. I was quite content to live by candlelight or lamplight. It lent a romantic glow to my writing life.

And a lot of romance went into those early stories. There was the girl on the train in 'The Eyes Are Not Here', and the girl selling baskets on the platform at Deoli, and Aunt Maram's amours behind the Dilaram Bazaar, and romantic episodes in places as unlikely as Shamli and Bijnor (Pipalnagar). However, as my intention is to give the reader a picture of Dehra as I knew it, the stories in this collection are all set in Dehra Dun and its immediate environs. I was writing for anyone who would read me. It was only much later that I began writing for children.

Some favourite places for my fictional milieu were the parade-ground or maidaan, the Paltan Bazaar and its offshoots, the lichee gardens of Dalanwala, the tea-gardens, the quiet upper reaches of the Rajpur Road (non-transformed into shopping malls), the sal forests near Rajpur, the approach to Dehra by road or rail, and of course the railway station which is much the same as it used to be.

When I was a boy, many of the bungalows (such as the one built by my grandfather) had fairly large grounds or compounds—flower gardens in front, orchards at the back. Apart from litchis, the common fruit trees were papaya, guava, mango, lemon, and the pomalo, a sort of grapefruit. Most of those large compounds have now been converted into housing-estates. Dehra's population has gone from fifty thousand in 1950 to over seven lakhs at present. Not much room left for fruit trees!

Some of the stories, such as 'A Handful of Nuts' and 'Living Without Money', were written long after I'd left Dehra, but I think the atmosphere of the place comes through quite strongly in them. When a writer looks back at a particular place or period in his life, he tries to capture the essence of the place and the experience.

During the two years I freelanced from Bibiji's flat (1956–58), I produced over thirty short stories, a couple of novellas and numerous articles of an ephemeral nature. I managed to sell some of the stories to the BBC's Home service programme—*The Thief, Night Train at Deoli, The Woman on Platform 8*—others to the *Elizabethan, Illustrated Weekly of India, Sunday Statesman* (over the years, a few have been lost.) In India, Rs 50 was the most you got for a short story or article, but you could live quite comfortably on three or four hundred rupees a month— provided your mode of transport was limited to the bicycle. Only successful businessmen and doctors owned cars.

My stepfather was an exception. He was an unsuccessful businessman who used a different car every month. That was because, before leaving Dehra, he ran a motor workshop, and if a car was left with him for repairs or overhauling ('oiling and greasing' he called it) he would use it for a month or two on the pretext of trying it out, before returning it to its owner. This he would do only when the owner's patience had reached its limit; sometimes the car had to be taken away by force. Occasionally my stepfather would relent and return the car of his own accord— along with a bill for having looked after it for so long!

His talents went unappreciated in Dehra. When he moved to Delhi he became a successful salesperson.

Some of the characters in my Dehra stories were fictional, some were based on real people; Granny was real, of course. And so were the boys in 'The Room' and 'Vagrants'. But did Rusty really make love to Meena Kapoor? It's a question I have often been asked and must leave unanswered. It might have happened. And then again, it might not. I prefer to leave it as a sweet mystery that will never be solved.

One thing is certain. Dehra played an integral part in my development as a writer. More than Shimla, where I did my schooling. More than London, where I lived for nearly four years. More than Delhi, where I spent a number of years. As much as Mussoorie, where I have passed half my life. It must have been the ambience of the place, something about it, that suited my temperament.

But it's a different place now, and no longer do I feel like 'singin' in the rain' as I walk down the Rajpur Road. I am in danger of being knocked down by a speeding vehicle if I try out my old song-and-dance routine. So I keep well to the side of the pavement and look out for known landmarks—an old peepal tree, a familiar corner, a surviving bungalow, a bookshop, the sabzi-mandi, a bit of wasteland where once we played cricket.

There was a wild flower, a weed, that grew all over Dehra and still does. We called it Blue Mint. It grows in ditches, in neglected gardens, anywhere there's a bit of open land. It's there nearly all the year round. I've always associated it with Dehra. The burgeoning human population has been unable to suppress it. This is one plant that will never go extinct. It refuses to go away. I have known it since I was a boy, and as long as it's there I shall know that a part of me still lives in Dehra.

BE PREPARED

I was a Boy Scout once, although I couldn't tell a slip knot from a granny knot, nor a reef knot from a thief knot. I did know that a thief knot was to be used to tie up a thief, should you happen to catch one. I have never caught a thief—and wouldn't know what to do with one since I can't tie the right knot. I'd just let him go with a warning, I suppose. And tell him to become a Boy Scout.

'Be prepared!' That's the Boy Scout motto. And it is a good one, too. But I never seem to be well prepared for anything, be it an exam or a journey or the roof blowing off my room. I get halfway through a speech and then forget what I have to say next. Or I make a new suit to attend a friend's wedding, and then turn up in my pyjamas.

So, how did I, the most impractical of boys, survive as a Boy Scout?

Well, it seems a rumour had gone around the junior school (I was still a junior then) that I was a good cook. I had never cooked anything in my life, but of course I had spent a lot of time in the tuck shop making suggestions and advising Chimpu, who ran the tuck shop, and encouraging him to make more and better samosas, jalebies, tikkees and pakoras. For my unwanted advice, he would favour me with an occasional free samosa. So, naturally, I looked upon him as a friend and benefactor. With this qualification, I was given a cookery badge and put in charge of our troop's supply of rations.

There were about twenty of us in our troop. During the summer break our Scoutmaster, Mr Oliver, took us on a camping expedition to Taradevi, a temple-crowned mountain a few miles outside Shimla. That first night we were put to work, peeling potatoes, skinning onions, shelling peas and pounding masalas. These various ingredients being ready, I was asked, as the troop cookery expert, what should be done with them.

'Put everything in that big degchi,' I ordered. 'Pour half a tin of ghee over the lot. Add some nettle leaves, and cook for half an hour.'

When this was done, everyone had a taste, but the general opinion was that the dish lacked something. 'More salt,' I suggested.

More salt was added. It still lacked something. 'Add a cup of sugar,' I ordered.

Sugar was added to the concoction, but it still lacked something.

'We forgot to add tomatoes,' said one of the Scouts. 'Never mind,' I said. 'We have tomato sauce. Add a bottle of tomato sauce!'

'How about some vinegar?' suggested another boy. 'Just the thing,' I said. 'Add a cup of vinegar!'

'Now it's too sour,' said one of the tasters.

'What jam did we bring?' I asked.

'Gooseberry jam.'

'Just the thing. Empty the bottle!'

The dish was a great success. Everyone enjoyed it, including Mr Oliver, who had no idea what had gone into it.

'What's this called?' he asked.

'It's an all-Indian sweet-and-sour jam-potato curry,' I ventured.

'For short, just call it Bond bhujjia,' said one of the boys. I had earned my cookery badge!

Poor Mr Oliver; he wasn't really cut out to be a Scoutmaster, any more than I was meant to be a Scout.

The following day, he told us he would give us a lesson in tracking. Taking a half-hour start, he walked into the forest, leaving behind him a trail of broken twigs, chicken feathers, pine cones and chestnuts. We were to follow the trail until we found him.

Unfortunately, we were not very good trackers. We did follow Mr Oliver's trail some way into the forest, but then we were distracted by a pool of clear water. It looked very inviting. Abandoning our uniforms, we jumped into the pool and had a great time romping about or just lying on its grassy banks and enjoying the sunshine. Many hours later, feeling hungry, we returned to our campsite and set about preparing the evening meal. It was Bond bhujjia again, but with a few variations.

It was growing dark, and we were beginning to worry about Mr Oliver's whereabouts when he limped into the camp, assisted by a couple of local villagers. Having waited for us at the far end of the forest for a couple of hours, he had decided to return by following his own trail, but in the gathering gloom he was soon lost. Village folk returning home from the temple took charge and escorted him back to the camp. He was very angry and made us return all our good-conduct and other badges, which he stuffed into his haversack. I had to give up my cookery badge.

An hour later, when we were all preparing to get into our sleeping bags for the night, Mr Oliver called out, 'Where's dinner?'

'We've had ours,' said one of the boys. 'Everything is finished, sir.'

'Where's Bond? He's supposed to be the cook. Bond, get up and make me an omelette.'

'I can't, sir.'

'Why not?'

'You have my badge. Not allowed to cook without it. Scout rule, sir.'

'I've never heard of such a rule. But you can take your badges, all of you. We return to school tomorrow.'

Mr Oliver returned to his tent in a huff.

But I relented and made him a grand omelette, garnishing it with dandelion leaves and a chilli.

'Never had such an omelette before,' confessed Mr Oliver.

'Would you like another, sir?'

'Tomorrow, Bond, tomorrow. We'll breakfast early tomorrow.'

But we had to break up our camp before we could do that because in the early hours of the next morning, a bear strayed into our camp, entered the tent where our stores were kept, and created havoc with all our provisions, even rolling our biggest degchi down the hillside.

In the confusion and uproar that followed, the bear entered Mr Oliver's tent (our Scoutmaster was already outside, fortunately) and came out entangled in his dressing gown. It then made off towards the forest, a comical sight in its borrowed clothes.

And though we were a troop of brave little scouts, we thought it better to let the bear keep the gown.

A LOVE OF LONG AGO

Last week, as the taxi took me to Delhi, I passed through the small town in the foothills where I had lived as a young man.

Well, it's the only road to Delhi and one must go that way, but I seldom travel beyond the foothills. As the years go by, my visits to the city—any city—are few and far between. But whenever I am on that road, I look out of the window of my bus or taxi, to catch a glimpse of the first-floor balcony where a row of potted plants lend colour to an old and decrepit building. Ferns, a palm, a few bright marigolds, zinnias and nasturtiums—they made that balcony stand out from others; it was impossible to miss it.

But last week, when I looked out of the taxi window, the balcony garden had gone. A few broken pots remained; but the ferns had crumpled into dust, the palm had turned brown and yellow, and of the flowers nothing remained.

All these years I had taken that balcony garden for granted, and now it had gone. It jerked me upright in my seat. I looked back at the building for signs of life, but saw none. The taxi sped on. On my way back, I decided, I would look again. But it was as though a part of my life had come to an abrupt end; a part that I had almost come to take for granted. The link between youth and middle age, the bridge that spanned that gap, had suddenly been swept away.

And what had happened to Kamla, I wondered. Kamla, who had tended those plants all these years, knowing I would be looking out for them even though I might not see her, even though she might never see me.

Chance gives, and takes away, and gives again. But I would have to look elsewhere now, for the memories of my love, my young love, the girl who came into my life for a few blissful weeks and then went out of it for the remainder of our lives.

Was it almost thirty years ago that it all happened? How old was I then? Twenty-two at the most! And Kamla could not have been more than seventeen.

She had a laughing face, mischievous, always ready to break into a smile or peals of laughter. Sparkling brown eyes. How can I ever forget those eyes? Peeping at me from behind a window curtain, following me as I climbed the steps to my room—the room that was separated from her quarters by a narrow wooden landing that creaked loudly if I tried to move quietly across it. The trick was to dash across, as she did so neatly on her butterfly feet.

She was always on the move—flitting about on the verandah, running errands of no consequence, dancing on the steps, singing on the rooftop as she hung out the family washing. Only once was she still. That was when we met on the steps in the dark, and I stole a kiss, a sweet phantom kiss. She was very still then, very close, a butterfly drawing out nectar, and then she broke away from me and ran away laughing.

'What is your work?' she asked me one day.

'I write stories.'

'Will you write one about me?'

'Some day.'

I was living in a room above Moti-Bibi's grocery shop near the cinema. At night I could hear the soundtrack from the films. The songs did not help me much with my writing, nor with my affair, for Kamla could not come out at night. We met in the afternoons when the whole town took a siesta and expected us to do the same. Kamla had a young brother who worked for Moti-Bibi (a widow who was also my landlady) and it was through the boy that I had first met Kamla.

Moti-Bibi always a sent me a glass of kanji or sugar-cane juice or lime-juice (depending on the season) around noon. Usually the boy brought me the drink, but one day I looked up from my typewriter to see what at first I thought was an apparition hovering over me. She seemed to shimmer before me in the hot sunlight that came slashing through the open door. I looked up into her face and our eyes met over the rim of the glass. I forgot to take it from her.

What I liked about her was her smile. It dropped over her face slowly, like sunshine moving over brown hills. She seemed to give out some of the glow that was in her face. I felt it pour over me. And this golden feeling did not pass when she left the room. That was how I knew she was going to mean something special to me.

They were poor, but in time I was to realize that I was even poorer. When I discovered that plans were afoot to marry her to a widower of forty, I plucked up enough courage to declare that I would marry her myself. But my youth was no consideration. The widower had land and a generous gift of money for Kamla's parents. Not only was this offer attractive; it was customary. What had I to offer? A small rented room, a typewriter and a precarious income of two to three hundred rupees a month from freelancing. I told the brother that I would be famous one day, that I would be rich, that I would be writing bestsellers! He did not believe me. And who can blame him? I never did write bestsellers or become rich. Nor did I have parents or relatives to speak on my behalf.

I thought of running away with Kamla. When I mentioned it to her, her eyes lit up. She thought it would be great fun. Women in love can be more reckless than men! But I had read too many stories about runaway marriages ending in disaster, and I lacked the courage to go through with such an adventure. I must have known instinctively that it would not work. Where would we go, and how would we live? There would be no home to crawl back to, for either of us.

Had I loved more passionately, more fiercely, I might have felt compelled to elope with Kamla, regardless of the consequences. But it never became an intense relationship. We had so few moments together. Always stolen moments—on the stairs, on the roof, in the deserted junkyard behind the shops. She seemed to enjoy every moment of this secret affair. I fretted and longed for something more permanent. Her responses, so sweet and generous, only made my longing greater. But she seemed content with the immediate moment and what it offered.

And so the marriage took place, and she did not appear to be too dismayed about her future. But before she left for her husband's house, she asked me for some of the plants that I had owned and nourished on my small balcony.

'Take them all,' I said. 'I am leaving, anyway.'
'Where are you going?'
'To Delhi—to find work. But I shall come this way sometimes.'
'My husband's house is on the Delhi road. You will pass that way. I will keep these flowers where you can see them.'

We did not touch each other in parting. Her brother came and collected the plants. Only the cacti remained. Not a lover's plant, the cactus! I gave the cacti to my landlady and went to live in Delhi.

◆

And whenever I passed through the old place, summer or winter, I looked out of the window of my bus or taxi and saw the garden flourishing on Kamla's balcony; leaf and fern abounded, and the flowers grew rampant on the sunny ledge.

Once I saw her, leaning over the balcony railing. I stopped the taxi and waved to her. She waved back, smiling like the sun breaking through clouds. She called to me to come up, but I said I would come another time. I never did visit her home, and I never saw her husband. Her parents had gone back to their village, her brother had vanished into the great grey spaces of India.

In recent years, after leaving Delhi and making my home in the hills, I have passed through the town less often; but the flowers have always been there, bright and glowing in their increasingly shabby surroundings. Except on this last journey of mine…

And on the return trip, only yesterday, I looked again, but the house was empty and desolate. I got out of the car and looked up at the balcony and called Kamla's name—called it after so many years—but there was no answer.

I asked questions in the locality. The old man had died, his wife had gone away, probably to her village. There had been no children. Would she return? No one could say. The house had been sold; it would be pulled down to make way for a block of flats.

I glanced once more at the deserted balcony, the withered, drooping plants. A butterfly flitted about the railing, looking in vain for a flower on which to alight. It settled briefly on my hand, before opening its wings and fluttering away into the blue.

THE FOUR FEATHERS

Our school dormitory was a very long room with about thirty beds, fifteen on either side of the room. This was good for pillow fights. Class V would take on class VII (the two senior classes in our prep-school) and there would be plenty of space for leaping, struggling small boys, pillows flying, feathers flying, until there was a cry of 'Here comes Fishy!' or 'Here comes Olly!' and either Mr Fisher, the headmaster, or Mr Oliver, the senior master, would come striding in, cane in hand, to put an end to the general mayhem. Pillow fights were allowed, up to a point; nobody got hurt. But parents sometimes complained if, at the end of the term, a boy came home with a pillow devoid of cotton-wool or feathers.

In that last year at prep-school in Simla, there were four of us who were close friends—Bimal, whose home was in Bombay; Riaz, who came from Lahore; Brian, who hailed from Vellore; and your narrator, who lived wherever his father (then in the Air Force) was posted.

We called ourselves 'four feathers'—the feathers signifying that we were companions in adventure, comrades in arms, knights of the round table, etc. Bimal adopted a peacock's feather as his emblem; he was always a bit showy. Riaz chose a falcon's feather—although we couldn't find one. Brian and I were at first offered crows or murghi feathers, but we protested vigorously and threatened a walk-out. Finally, I settled for a parrot's feather (taken from Mr Fisher's pet parrot) and Brian found a woodpecker's, which suited him, as he was always knocking things about.

Bimal was all thin legs and arms, so light and frisky that at times he seemed to be walking on air. We called him 'Bambi', after the delicate little deer in the Disney film. Riaz, on the other hand, was a sturdy boy, good at games but not very studious; but always good-natured, always smiling. Brian was a dark, good-looking boy from the South; he was just a little spoilt—hated being given out in a cricket match and would refuse to leave the crease!—but he was affectionate and a loyal friend. I was the 'scribe'—good at inventing stories in order to get out of scrapes—but hopeless at sums, my highest marks being 22 out of 100.

On Sunday afternoons, when there were no classes or organized games, we were allowed to roam about on the hillside below the school. The four feathers would laze about on the short summer grass, sharing the occasional food parcel from home, reading comics (sometimes a book) and making plans for the long winter holidays. My father, who collected everything from stamps to sea-shells to butterflies, had given me a butterfly-net and urged me to try and catch a rare species which, he said, was found only near Chotta Simla. He described it as a large purple butterfly with yellow and black borders on its wings. A 'Purple Emperor', I think it was called. As I wasn't very good at identifying butterflies, I would chase anything that happened to flit across the school grounds, usually ending up with common 'red admirals', 'clouded yellows' or 'cabbage whites'. But that 'Purple Emperor'—that rare specimen being sought by collectors the world over—proved elusive. I would have to seek my fortune in some other line of endeavour.

One day, scrambling about among the rocks and thorny bushes below the school, I almost fell over a small bundle lying in the shade of a young spruce tree. On taking a closer look, I discovered that the bundle was really a baby, wrapped up in a tattered old blanket.

'Feathers, feathers!' I called, 'come here and look. A baby's been left here!'

The feathers joined me, and we all stared down at the infant, who was fast asleep.

'Who would leave a baby on the hillside?' asked Bimal of no one in particular.

'Someone who doesn't want it,' said Brian.

'And hoped some good people would come along and keep it,' said Riaz.

'A panther might have come along instead,' I said. 'Can't leave it here.'

'Well, we'll just have to adopt it,' said Bimal.

'We can't adopt a baby,' said Brian.

'Why not?'

'We have to be married.'

'We don't.'

'Not us, you dope. The grown-ups who adopt babies.'

'Well, we can't just leave it here for grown-ups to come along,' I said.

'We don't even know if it's a boy or a girl,' said Riaz.

'Makes no difference. A baby's a baby. Let's take it back to school.'

'And keep it in the dormitory?'

'Of course not. Who's going to feed it? Babies need milk. We'll hand it over to Mrs Fisher. She doesn't have a baby.'

'Maybe she doesn't want one. Look, it's beginning to cry. Let's hurry!'

Riaz picked up the wide-awake and crying baby and gave it to Bimal who gave it to Brian who gave it to me. The four feathers marched up the hill to school with a very noisy baby.

'Now it has done potty in the blanket,' I complained, 'and some of it is on my shirt.'

'Never mind,' said Bimal. 'It's in a good cause. You're a Boy Scout, remember. You're supposed to help people in distress.'

The headmaster and his wife were in their drawing-room, enjoying their afternoon tea and cakes. We trudged in, and Bimal announced, 'We've got something for Mrs Fisher.'

Mrs Fisher took a look at the bundle in my arms and let out a shriek. 'What have you brought here, Bond?'

'A baby ma'am. I think it's a girl. Do you want to adopt it?'

Mrs Fisher threw up her arms in consternation, and turned to her husband. 'What are we to do, Frank? These boys are impossible. They've picked up someone's child!'

'We'll have to inform the police,' said Mr Fisher, reaching for the telephone, 'we can't have lost babies in the school.'

Just then there was a commotion outside, and a wild-eyed woman, her clothes disheveled, entered at the front door accompanied by several men-folk from one of the villages. She ran towards us, crying out, 'My baby, my baby! *Mera bachcha!* You've stolen my baby!'

'We found it on the hillside,' I stammered.

'That's right,' said Brian. 'Finders keepers!'

'Quiet, Adams,' said Mr Fisher, holding up his hand for order and addressing the villagers in a friendly manner. 'These boys found the baby alone on the hillside and brought it here before...before...'

'Before the hyaenas got it,' I put in.

'Quite right, Bond. And why did you leave your child alone?' he asked the woman.

'I put her down for five minutes so that I could climb the plum tree and collect the plums. When I came down, the baby had gone! But I could hear it crying up on the hill. I called the men-folk and we came here looking for it.'

'Well, here's your baby,' I said, thrusting it into her arms. By then I was glad to be rid of it! 'Look after it properly in future.'

'Kidnapper!' she screamed at me.

Mr Fisher succeeded in mollifying the villagers. 'These boys are good scouts,' he told them. 'It's their business to help people.'

'Scout's Law Number Three, Sir,' I added. 'To be useful and helpful.'

And then the headmaster turned the tables on the villagers. 'By the way, these plum trees belong to the school. So do the peaches and apricots. Now I know why they've been disappearing so fast!'

The villagers, a little chastened, went their way. Mr Fisher reached for his cane. From the way he fondled it I knew he was itching to use it on our bottoms.

'No, Frank,' said Mrs Fisher, intervening on our behalf. 'It was really very sweet of them to look after that baby. And look at Bond—he's got baby-goo all over his clothes.'

'So he has. Go and take a bath, all of you. And what are you grinning about, Bond?' asked Mr Fisher.

'Scout's Law Number Eight, Sir. A scout smiles and whistles under all difficulties.'

And so ended the first adventure of the four feathers.

HERE COMES MR OLIVER

Apart from being our Scoutmaster, Mr Oliver taught us maths, a subject in which I had some difficulty obtaining pass marks. Sometimes I scraped through; usually I got something like twenty or thirty out of a hundred. 'Failed again, Bond,' Mr Oliver would say. 'What will you do when you grow up?'
'Become a scoutmaster, sir.'
'Scoutmasters don't get paid. It's an honorary job. You could become a cook. That would suit you.' He hadn't forgotten our Scout camp, when I had been the camp's cook.

If Mr Oliver was in a good mood, he'd give me grace marks, passing me by a mark or two. He wasn't a hard man, but he seldom smiled. He was very dark, thin, stooped (from a distance he looked like a question mark) and balding. He was about forty, still a bachelor and it was said that he had been unlucky in love—that the girl he was going to marry jilted him at the last moment, running away with a sailor while Mr Oliver waited at the church, ready for the wedding ceremony. No wonder he always had such a sorrowful look.

Mr Oliver did have one inseparable companion: a dachshund, a snappy little 'sausage' of a dog, who looked upon the human race, and especially small boys, with a certain disdain and frequent hostility. We called him Hitler. (This was 1945, and the dictator was at the end of his tether.) He was impervious to overtures of friendship, and if you tried to pat or stroke him he would do his best to bite your fingers or your shin or ankle. However, he was devoted to Mr Oliver and followed him everywhere except into the classroom; this our Headmaster would not allow. You remember that old nursery rhyme:

Mary had a little lamb,
Its fleece was white as snow,
And everywhere that Mary went
The lamb was sure to go.

Well, we made up our own version of the rhyme, and I must confess to having had a hand in its composition. It went like this:

Olly had a little dog,
It was never out of sight,
And everyone that Olly met
The dog was sure to bite!

It followed him about the school grounds. It followed him when he took a walk through the pines to the Brockhuist tennis courts. It followed him into town and home again. Mr Oliver had no other friend, no other companion. The dog slept at the foot of Mr Oliver's bed. It did not sit at the breakfast table, but it had buttered toast for breakfast and soup and crackers for dinner. Mr Oliver had to take his lunch in the dining hall with the staff and boys, but he had an arrangement with one of the bearers whereby a plate of dal, rice and chapattis made its way to Mr Oliver's quarters and his well-fed pet.

And then tragedy struck.

Mr Oliver and Hitler were returning to school after an evening walk through the pines. It was dusk, and the light was fading fast. Out of the shadows of the trees emerged a lean and hungry panther. It pounced on the hapless dog, flung it across the road, seized it between its powerful jaws and made off with its victim into the darkness of the forest.

Mr Oliver was untouched but frozen into immobility for at least a minute. Then he began calling for help. Some bystanders, who had witnessed the incident, began shouting too. Mr Oliver ran into the forest, but there was no sign of dog or panther.

Mr Oliver appeared to be a broken man. He went about his duties with a poker face, but we could all tell that he was grieving for his lost companion, for in the classroom he was listless and indifferent to whether or not we followed his calculations on the blackboard. In times of personal loss, the Highest Common Factor made no sense.

Mr Oliver was no longer seen going on his evening walk. He stayed in his room, playing cards with himself. He played with his food, pushing most of it aside. There were no chapattis to send home.

'Olly needs another pet,' said Bimal, wise in the ways of adults.

'Or a wife,' said Tata, who thought on those lines.

'He's too old. He must be over forty.'

'A pet is best,' I said. 'What about a parrot?'

'You can't take a parrot for a walk,' said Bimal. 'Olly wants someone to walk beside him.'

'A cat maybe.'

'Hitler hated cats. A cat would be an insult to Hitler's memory.'

'Then he needs another dachshund. But there aren't any around here.'

'Any dog will do. We'll ask Chimpu to get us a pup.'

Chimpu ran the tuck shop. He lived in the Chotta Shimla bazaar, and occasionally we would ask him to bring us tops or marbles, a comic or other little things that we couldn't get in school. Five of us Boy Scouts contributed a rupee each, which we gave to Chimpu and asked him to get us a pup. 'A good breed,' we told him, 'not a mongrel.'

The next evening Chimpu turned up with a pup that seemed to be a combination of at least five different breeds, all good ones no doubt. One ear lay flat, the other stood upright. It was spotted like a Dalmatian, but it had the legs of a spaniel and the tail of a Pomeranian. It was floppy and playful, and the tail wagged a lot, which was more than Hitler's ever did.

'It's quite pretty,' said Tata. 'Must be a female.'

'He may not want a female,' said Bimal.

'Let's give it a try,' I said.

'During our play hour, before the bell rang for supper, we left the pup on the steps outside Mr Oliver's front door. Then we knocked, and sped into the hibiscus bush that lined the pathway.

Mr Oliver opened the door. He looked down at the pup with an expressionless face. The pup began to paw at Mr Oliver's shoes, loosening one of his laces in the process.

'Away with you!' muttered Mr Oliver. 'Buzz off!' And he pushed the pup away, gently but firmly, and closed the door.

We went through the same procedure again, but the result was much the same. We now had a playful pup on our hands, and Chimpu had gone home for the night. We would have to conceal it in the dormitory.

At first we hid it in Bimal's locker, but it began to yelp and struggled to get out. Tata took it into the shower room, but it wouldn't stay there either. It began running around the dormitory, playing with socks, shoes, slippers and anything else it could get hold of.

'Watch out!' hissed one of the boys. 'Here comes Fisher!'

Mrs Fisher, the Headmaster's wife, was on her nightly rounds, checking to make sure we were all in bed and not up to some natural mischief. I grabbed the pup and hid it under my blanket. It was quiet there, happy to nibble at my toes. When Mrs Fisher had gone, I let the pup loose again and for the rest of the night it had the freedom of the dormitory.

At the crack of dawn, before first light, Bimal and I sped out of the dormitory in our pyjamas, taking the pup with us. We banged hard on Mr Oliver's door, and kept knocking until we heard footsteps approaching. As soon as the door was slowly opened, we pushed the pup inside and ran for our lives.

Mr Oliver came to class as usual, but there was no pup with him. Three or four days passed, and still no sign of the pup! Had he passed it on to someone else, or simply let it wander off on its own?

'Here comes Olly!' called Bimal, from our vantage point near the school bell.

Mr Oliver was setting out for his evening walk. He was carrying a strong walnut-wood walking stick—to keep panthers at bay, no doubt. He looked neither left nor right and if he noticed us watching him, Mr Oliver gave no sign. But then, scurrying behind him was the pup! The creature of many good breeds was accompanying Mr Oliver on his walk. It had been well brushed and was wearing a bright red collar. Like Mr Oliver, it took no notice of us. It walked along beside its new master.

Mr Oliver and the little pup were soon inseparable companions, and my friends and I were quite pleased with ourselves. Mr Oliver gave absolutely no indication that he knew where the pup had come from, but when the end-of-term exams were over, and Bimal and I were sure that we had failed our maths papers, we were surprised to find that we had passed after all—with grace marks!

'Good old Olly!' said Bimal. 'So he knew all the time.' Tata, of course, did not need grace marks—he was a wizard at maths—but Bimal and I decided we would thank Mr Oliver for his kindness.

'Nothing to thank me for,' said Mr Oliver gruffly, but with a twist at the corners of his mouth, which was the nearest he came to a smile. 'I've seen enough of you two in junior school. It's high time you went up to the senior school—and God help you there!'